GIANTS

Liminal Books is an imprint of Between the Lines Publishing. The Liminal Books name and logo are trademarks of Between the Lines Publishing.

Cover design by Morgan Bliadd

Between the Lines Publishing
1769 Lexington Ave N., Ste 286
Roseville, MN 55113
btwnthelines.com

Published: March 2024

Original ISBN (Paperback) 978-1-958901-78-6

Original ISBN (eBook) 978-1-958901-79-3

Passages adopted from The Epic of Gilgamesh, 'Standard' Akkadian version, tablet 1, circa 13th - 10th Century BCE.

GIANTS

James W. White

For Steffi and Sheldon

Prologue

By 1750 the Age of The Enlightenment dominated
the world of ideas throughout Europe. Questions about
the origins of life, man's relationship with the world
around him, and the cosmos were openly discussed and
debated for the first time.

Many of these conversations stemmed from the
observations, rumors, and stories that came back from
the first known circumnavigation of the world,
accomplished over two hundred years previously, by a
fleet of five small ships under the command of the
Portuguese nobleman and navigator, Ferdinand
Magellan. Very few physical specimens made it back to
Europe. However, a collection of meticulous notes,

maintained by Magellan's assistant, Antonio Pigafetta, survived the journey.

Pigafetta's chronicles included an incident that occurred along the southern coast of South America, a region that later became known as Patagonia. During a layover, Pigafetta wrote about sighting a population of giant apes living near the ships' anchorage.

The news created a firestorm of controversy when it reached Europe. For the Right Honorable James Burnett, Lord Monboddo, Justice of the High Court of Edinburgh, as well as a noted naturalist, deist, and freethinker, the sensational news became a personal issue when his daughter, Elizabeth Burnett, launched a scientific expedition to Patagonia to investigate Pigafetta's claims.

Giants opens when Elizabeth's expedition has been cut short by a mutiny. After a deadly encounter with a band of cutthroats, she and her colleagues are cast adrift on a longboat and left to die on the open sea. After three days, they are shipwrecked on a desolate shore without provisions and hundreds of miles from any known habitation.

Chapter One

The wave carried us high on its crest until our longboat crashed against an exposed reef. Water cascaded over the bow's splintered remains, forcing the boat downward.

"Och God, we're sinking!" Elizabeth cried out. A cloak of fog hid all landmarks as we lumbered our way into a dark maelstrom of crashing water. Other cries rang out when the wreckage we sat in spun through an eddy and bashed broadside against another rock.

"Grab hold!" Henry reached out toward the looming wall of rock. Five pairs of hands felt for purchase along its seaweed-covered surface. There was none. Barnacles scraped and bloodied our hands as we were pulled back with the ebb.

Wallowing now, half full of water, what was left of our boat made a second rush landward, stern first, with the next wave. The stern, still relatively intact, lodged itself in a narrow defile between outcroppings and held against the receding current.

"Make haste!" Henry jumped overboard and stood waist-deep in the churning water. He held on to the gunwale and struggled against the surge. "We must be close to shore," he shouted.

We all pitched into the water in the lull between waves and scrambled to reach dry land before we were swept to watery graves. The few supplies and possessions we had were left behind. Larger rocks appeared in the mist as we crossed tide pools.

Elizabeth found shelter on a protected patch of sand and held up a hand. "Let me take a coont," she ordered in the confident, self-assured tone we all knew well. The rest of us gathered around her, like unhappy spirits shivering in the cold morning mist.

"John," she shouted over the sound of the waves.

"Aye." I raised my hand. Watery streaks on my spectacles distorted my surroundings. I had no means to clean them, and I had no strength to make an additional comment.

"Jacob."

"Aye," came the reply. Jacob clutched his right arm, where the sleeve of his tunic was ripped open. Blood trickled through his fingers, down to the sand at his feet. Jacob didn't complain, but his wound needed attention. I was too overcome by our ordeal to care. Unfortunately, our medicine chest was at the bottom of the sea.

"Roger..."

There was no response. I looked around and made out his figure standing silently.

Elizabeth waited a minute and tried again. "Roger, please respond when I cry yer name."

"Aye," Roger muttered. "But rather than coonting noses, should we nae..."

Elizabeth cut him off with a shake of her head. "Henry."

"Cheers," Henry waved a cheerful hello. "Begging your pardon, Elizabeth, my dear, I do not recall this stop on the expedition's itinerary. Is this a surprise destination ye have been keeping from us?"

Elizabeth stifled a smile. Jacob and I also shared a grin.

"This is neither the time nor the place tae play court jester." Roger glared at Henry and straightened his stance to his full height. His sour tone smothered our moment of levity.

"This isn't the time nor place for brooding either."

Henry's voice dropped an octave. "Wherever this is, we got out of a tight spot to live another day."

Roger leaned over and spat seawater in the sand. Water ran out his nose in a gush and he tried to hide the indignity with a handkerchief. "Nae thanks to ye. Sassenach dobber."

"I beg your pardon." Henry approached Roger, his fists clenched. I backed away to avoid incurring any collateral damage if it came to that.

Sounding like an exasperated headmaster, Elizabeth muttered something under her breath and, with a surprisingly graceful jump, put herself between Roger and Henry. Although tall for a woman, physically she was no match for the enraged brutes, but in terms of courage, she was a force to be reckoned with. I admired her strong personality and intelligence. Even dressed in rags she was a bonnie lass.

I have no right to covet her affections, an older man with a wife, for goodness sake, but I have often found myself acting like an infatuated schoolboy in her company. I occasionally take the liberty of calling her Beth, a term of endearment that I have no right to claim, yet she tolerates my impropriety. To be sure, men can be such loathsome creatures.

"Gentlemen, please," Elizabeth barked. "We canna afford the luxury of pride nor that of honor. Put yer arrogance tae work on our predicament. That should be challenging enough for the both o ye."

Roger and Henry continued glaring at each other, but they backed off. I suspect they were relieved not to engage in anything more physical.

All of us now accounted for, I stood shivering in a patch of sunlight and waited for the full sun while our ordeal raced through my mind. A bloody insurrection by a swarm of brigands aboard our ship, , The Cumberland, had taken the lives of the captain and two of our colleagues. The rest of us were forced overboard into a longboat. Will word ever get back to Scotland? Three days of aimless drifting in the open ocean had left us dehydrated and weak, and now this, shipwrecked on the eastern shore of South America, approximately forty-six degrees south latitude, with scant chance of rescue. Our instruments lost, and our hopes for a brilliant scientific expedition dashed forever.

The morning fog gave way to a fantastical landscape unlike anything I'd seen before. Tall crags, cliffs, and high, snow-covered peaks filled our view to the west.

"I see waterfalls." Jacob nodded toward clouds of mist rising from a pinnacle.

Roger pointed to a meandering strip of green that led to the ocean. "There be fresh water nearby."

To our left and right, a dry, brown shelf separated

the ocean from a vast chain of ragged peaks called a cordillera by the Spaniards. Aside from the green strip, there was no vegetation in either direction. No trees, no structures, no sign of habitation. Behind us, the endless ocean stretched to the eastern horizon.

The warming sun left our skin red and salty. Elizabeth pointed toward the stream and gestured for Jacob to follow her. "Is anyone else injured?"

I complained of a twisted ankle. But aside from Jacob's arm and a few scrapes and bruises, there were no other injuries.

Jacob held his wound tight and the blood flow lessened but didn't stop. "'Twas a piece of driftwood stuck in the rocks," he said. "Caught my arm right after I jumped. I wasna even aware it was bleeding until we got ashore."

"It doesna seem tae be a deep cut," Elizabeth said. "But we should rinse it in fresh water tae be sure." She walked slowly, waiting for Jacob to catch up. "Have we any medical supplies tae close the wound?"

Roger and I checked our pockets in vain. Henry's eyebrows arched up when he searched his pockets like he had found something, but he said nothing.

I wondered what he was hiding. Food? A note? I honored his privacy and held my tongue. The only Englishman among us, Henry could be mysterious at times, and a man of many secrets, yet often he was almost childish in his open-faced, naive behavior. I had nothing to offer but felt compelled to make some sort of contribution. "Perhaps we can find a bone splinter and tie a length of thread from some clothing?"

Elizabeth shook her head. "'Tis a worthy consideration, John." She held out her arm. "'Til such a time as we can fashion a needle substitute, rip off this sleeve and we'll use it as a bandage."

I hesitated, not wanting to damage what little protection Elizabeth had from the sun.

"Wait." Jacob shook his head. "I can manage. We need nae sacrifice articles of clothing just yet."

"That willna be necessary." Roger handed Elizabeth his kerchief. "I'm only too glad tae save our leader the shame of exposing herself unnecessarily."

"Och!" Elizabeth snapped as she bound Jacob's arm. "A scaly, wrinkled arm is hardly indecent exposure."

While we walked along the shoreline toward the stream, we left a trail of blood behind us.

Not a good sign. I hoped it wasn't a bad omen.

The few stands of brush along the stream bed offered little protection from the sun, but the cold, sweet water was all we wanted. Elizabeth dropped to her knees and plunged her head into a pool. Her red hair waved across the water. I busied myself with my refreshment to keep my eyes off our leader's unladylike conduct.

Beth had given up her feminine airs months ago when we left the Firth of Forth behind on a sunny day in October 1750, with streamers flying and bands playing at the edge of Leith Docks. My Mary was there, waving and clutching her sunbonnet, trying to hide her tears. But the most important person, Beth's faither, The Right Honorable James Burnett, Lord Monboddo, Justice of the High Court of Edinburgh, was nowhere to be seen.

"A publicity stunt," he had called it when she explained how, with Henry's assistance, she had convinced a group of investors to sponsor her expedition in return for exclusive rights to all artifacts and specimens that substantiate proof of the giants' existence, including captive apes themselves.

"An insufferable cad," was his assessment of her financial partner, Henry Wadsworth. "He and his associates have nae scientific interests; they are merely looking for curiosities from which to profit."

When Roger Ambrose and I left Justice Burnett's academic staff to join Elizabeth's expedition, Burnett blamed his daughter for hindering his work. Another defector, and one of Burnett's best scientific illustrators, Jacob Charles was a particular sore point.

My colleague, Roger, wouldn't stop talking about

how keen he was to join in the expedition. I was not so enthusiastic. The ordeal of a long sea voyage coupled with the unimaginable challenges of exploring uncharted territory on foot was not appealing. Being the ripe old age of two score and five, and in frail physical condition, gave me reason to believe that I would be more of a liability than an asset, despite my training and experience in the botanic and anatomical sciences. Also, I had my wife to think about. A prolonged absence would be a severe hardship for her.

Nonetheless, Elizabeth was persuasive and generous in compensation for Mary's isolation. I wasn't a hard sell. Alas, I dare say, I gave in to her flattery, and my own vanity. The opportunity to participate in exploring and possibly discovering whole new species of animals and plants was also hard to pass up, despite Doctor Burnett's arguments to the contrary.

"Aside from Pigafetta's hasty scribbles, there is nae a shred of evidence that Magellan encountered any so-called giants," Doctor Burnett announced at our farewell party the night before we set sail. "Yea waste good coin as well as putting the lives o talented men in danger, nae tae mention yer own," he stated when Elizabeth said goodbye the next day and climbed in her carriage. "Whoever heard of a woman leading an expedition anywhere?" he shouted while she slammed the carriage door. "Much less tae the far side o the world!"

While we drove to Leith Docks, along Bernard Street to Constitution Street, I fear I harbored doubts about Elizabeth's ambitious plans. Yet there I was, a committed participant, trotting off to an uncertain fate.

When we got on board the Cumberland and waved to the crowd, Philip, Elizabeth's betrothed, stood at the end of the pier, waving, and blowing kisses to Elizabeth, who was dressed in her specially made sailing costume. "I will be here tae celebrate yer triumphant return," he'd shouted, repeating what he had told her at one of her faither's scholarly suppers.

Lord Monboddo enjoyed exploring radical philosophies such as anthropology and evolutionary theory. Theories based on the philosopher Descartes' reflections on providing a naturalistic explanation of the origins of living beings. Monboddo was famous for his salons held in the company of his friends Robert Burns and Samuel Johnson and other luminaries at his home on St. John Street. There were detractors, of course. Hard line Evangelic groups, led by rogue ministers such as Ebenezer Erskine and John Barclay, voiced strong dissent to Monboddo's heretical theories. However, Monboddo's position as Judge of the Scottish Court of Session kept his dissidents at bay. Or so he thought.

A week before our departure, a lively debate had

erupted during one of Monboddo's salons about the question of man's relationship to other primates. Out of the corner of my eye, I saw Philip deftly excuse himself from the table and whisk Elizabeth upstairs, the skirts of her silk and taffeta gown swishing as they made their escape. She told me later that was when he had promised to marry her upon her return.

Now, half a world away from silk and taffeta and dressed in filthy woolen breeks, a blouse, and a leather jerkin, Beth sighed with relief as the cold water washed down her face and neck. Without a shred of embarrassment, she let the water expose the contours of her modest bosom.

"Bleeding can be such a nuisance," Roger said while helping Elizabeth wash Jacob's wound.

Roger leered at Elizabeth's front while poor Jacob groaned through the ordeal. I admit that my thoughts were less than innocent, yet I couldn't help but be revolted by Roger's conspicuous disregard for simple courtesies. But who was I to feel jealous? My arthritic joints, weak eyes, and fragile frame made it obvious that I would be the first if anyone were going to die in this unforgiving spot.

To break my worrisome train of thought, I ambled upstream and found Henry squatting beside a pool, bare chested, rinsing the sand out of his tunic. "It occurred tae me ye spoke with Captain Conrad when he took the noon sighting on Thursday, just before everything went tae hell. Did he mention our position?"

Henry took his time, carefully wringing out the garment. He had told me during the voyage the tunic was a present from a friend he knew from his days at Cambridge. "Yes," he replied. "'Twas the 4th of December. The sighting put us at the fortieth parallel south, about twelve hundred leagues south of Buenos Aires, probably more."

A rustling caught my attention. Jacob stood nearby, the arm bandage was already tinged with red. "I remember Captain Conrad told us the settlement at Puerto Santa Cruz is near the fiftieth parallel," Jacob said. "That means we must be at least seven hundred miles north."

"That is correct," Henry replied. "The three days we spent drifting influences our actual position, but regardless, I suspect we are a long way from either known point of habitation."

Jacob and I both stared at the empty ocean, now smooth as glass. "We are indeed hopelessly lost," Jacob whispered.

Henry smiled. "As my father used to say, it could be worse, we could be on fire." He splashed water over his head. Beads of water ran down his torso, glistening in the sunlight. "We should think of our lot as an adventure, not a disaster. I daresay, the land looks uninhabited, but maybe the inhabitants just don't leave a recognizable trace of their presence, heh?" He gave me a questioning look.

I turned my eyes away, not wishing to argue.

"Roger, I've had enough. Now please leave off." Elizabeth's voice had a shrill edge to it when she walked up to us with Roger following her. Her garments had dried quickly under the bright sun.

Roger's red face was more than sunburned, and he followed Elizabeth like a convict. When he reached the three of us, his hangdog expression made it clear he had, yet again, overstepped the bounds of propriety.

Henry quickly donned his tunic.

"Did I hear ye say something about our location?" Elizabeth stood next to Jacob and me, out of Roger's reach.

"Bad news, I'm afraid," I replied.

"Nae unexpected, though," Jacob added. "We all knew it was at least another two weeks sail tae our destination."

We stood quietly for a moment, each of us lost in thought, as we pondered the enormity of our plight.

"May I offer a suggestion?" Henry piped up. "I propose we bolster our spirits with some productive activity. We should split up into teams and explore our new home."

"This is *nae* my home," Roger snapped back.

Henry ignored Roger's retort and pointed at Beth and Jacob. "You go north, John and Roger, go south. Priorities are food, shelter, and firewood. I will investigate what is left of the boat."

"I willna take orders from ye," Roger grumbled. "Ye have nae authority over us." Roger glanced at Elizabeth for acknowledgement while she preoccupied herself adjusting Jacob's bandage.

Henry continued. "We'll meet back in that field of boulders from whence we came," he pointed toward the edge of the shoreline.

I was content to follow orders and scanned the southern landscape looking for a path.

"I believe Henry's idea is a good one. Let us begin." Elizabeth held Jacob's good arm gingerly. The two moved slowly, following open spaces and gaps in the rocky landscape.

From the way he walked, I could tell the bleeding sapped Jacob's strength and I worried he would suffer from the exercise.

We had been caught off guard when Peter and his men burst into the great cabin. Jacob had been the only one to stand up to them. He grabbed a cutlass and slashed at one of them, leaving the man moaning in a pool of blood. Jacob single-handedly turned a rout into a standoff. His bravery forced them to negotiate, and using Henry's money as a bargaining chip, he saved us from being fed to the sharks. Now, he had been maimed by the unforgiving hand of fate. Just like the expedition. Elizabeth's years of study, planning, and resources had come to this – five castaways with no hope of rescue and fearing death at any moment.

Jacob leaned on Elizabeth as he shuffled ahead. "Ye look high, and I will look low," I heard him say. "The moment we catch sight of a plate of roast beef with neeps and tatties, we should turn around."

Once they were out of sight, I walked south, favoring my right ankle. I wanted to sympathize with Roger, for we had been colleagues at Lord Monboddo's house and the Royal Society. Still, his behavior towards Elizabeth since we left Scotland had become unconscionable and I saw no reason for his antagonistic attitude toward Henry.

"There is nae point in challenging Henry," I said after Roger caught up. "As Elizabeth said, we need everyone's help noo. When Peter and his men killed Captain Conrad, I figured he'd kill us all. Ye must admit Henry used his money tae its best advantage, saving us from certain death."

Roger laughed. "Negotiating us into a longboat without a sail or even an oar, leaving us at the mercy o the ocean is nae my idea o saving anything."

I wiped my spectacles with my filthy kerchief and scanned the terrain around us. "At least we have our lives."

"Aye, but I wonder for how long." With that, Roger dismissed me with a shrug.

Chapter Two

Elizabeth and Jacob's voices came back across the still landscape. Elizabeth sounded excited. The two of them were clambering over a promontory of exposed rock. Elizabeth first, then Jacob, struggling to keep up.

"Elizabeth and Jacob seem tae be on tae something," I said.

The temperature was rising, making it hard to concentrate. Shimmering heat thermals rose like a curtain around us. High above us, a kettle of vultures circled, riding a thermal. "Nae yet," I mumbled. Feeling faint from the heat, I was about to head back when Roger bent and studied the ground at his feet. "By Jove," he said.

"What is it?"

Roger squatted down and looked closer. "I believe 'tis a track o some sort."

Indeed, there appeared to be a passageway cutting through clumps of vegetation. Impressions in the sand looked to be animal, but some were distinctively a human's foot. Footprints of various sizes pointed in both directions. "I am nae a tracker," Roger admitted, "but I would guess people have been here in the nae-to-distant past."

My discomfort was forgotten. "We should follow them."

The track seemed to go on forever. After following it for a hundred yards without finding any more discoveries, we returned to the boulders where Henry was unloading an armful of driftwood. Next to the woodpile was an assortment of tins, bottles, and pieces of broken glass. "The boat broke up among the rocks and what was left fell to the bottom of a pool. The tide is flooding, and I could only retrieve a few supplies. But there appears to be more. I'll go back at slack tide and try again." He looked at us for praise but got none.

Elizabeth appeared with Jacob slowly in tow. The kerchief around Jacob's arm was saturated. "We had better get ye back tae the stream and clean yer wound," Elizabeth said. Her face was flushed, eyes sparkling. I knew she was keeping something from us.

Jacob offered a weak smile. "I can manage it myself," he said and excused himself.

After Jacob left, Henry pulled something from inside his tunic. "I found this, Elizabeth. Something of yours, I believe." He held a brooch in the palm of his hand. An inscription on the cover read, 'October 12, 1750. To my dear daughter. May this wee token always stay safely next to ye. Yer father, James Burnett.'

Elizabeth clutched the brooch to her breast and allowed herself a sniffle. She trusted Henry in spite of his sometimes-flippant behavior. He had sold a lucrative import/export business to fund her expedition. When he had offered his services as a participant, she was grateful. He had no scientific experience. Still, I knew she was attracted to him and his stories of adventure during his service as a military officer with the British East India Company. But he never took the bait, unwilling even to joust with her in the flirtatious banter of young sophisticates. It was apparent to me he was a sodomite. It being a capital offense in our silly, backward culture, he had learned to hide his preferences, but subtle mannerisms gave him away.

"This brooch proves all is nae quite lost," she said. "Thank ye most sincerely, Henry."

There was no question about Roger's sexual

persuasion. He scowled, watching the two of them. "We have found something," he said, changing the subject.

"Wait," Elizabeth beamed. "Before ye tell us, follow me."

As we passed the stream, Henry shouted to Jacob. "When you are done, would you go back to the boulders and make a fire? We will return shortly. Use the flint I found to light some dry sprigs."

Jacob nodded without looking up, the wet kerchief still wrapped around his wound. The blood flow had not lessened, and I wondered if his condition could be something other than it appeared.

The heat of the day was over when we reached Elizabeth's discovery site, and long shadows stretched across the shelf of land Henry had called our new home. In front of us stood a field of conical hills, each about ten feet across and at least six feet high. They appeared to consist of discarded bones, pieces of hides, shells, and all manner of debris. There were also blackened depressions that looked like burn pits.

"Somebody had a feast." I held up broken pieces of earthenware, then let them fall through my fingers. "But left naught for us."

Henry inspected a pit and sifted through ashes and clumps of blackened bits. There was no evidence of a fire for months, maybe years.

"Hudson wrote about this practice during his exploration o the North American continent. I remember reading about it when I was a wee lass." Elizabeth walked around one of the hills, examining its details. "They are called shell mounds, common tae many American Indian cultures. They indicate the location o a ceremonial or burial place, depending on the tribe's customs. People have been here, gentlemen."

Henry squatted next to me while I was examining some bone fragments. "You are the biologist," Henry whispered. "See anything human?"

A thin, canine-looking tooth caught my eye. "Nae so far," I said. "Everything is ground up. Nae many specimens are big enough tae identify. The few teeth I have seen all appear tae be animal. They might be useful as a substitute needle with a little shaping, as I mentioned earlier." I stowed the tooth and two wee bones with tapered ends in my breast pocket.

Henry left my side and attacked a mound with his bare hands. Shells and bits of bone were scattered everywhere. "Maybe there is food stored inside these things."

Agitated by his disregard for the monuments, I stood and raised my voice. "Ye be desecrating the site, Henry. We take the chance o upsetting whoever lives here."

Henry paused. "Upset natives, you say? Bloody unlikely. What is there to get upset about? 'Tis all castaways and refuse. A dump, if you ask me."

Frustrated, I shook my head and tried to stifle my anger by moving away from Henry's senseless behavior. The man had no knowledge about aboriginal societal customs. Such ignorance might cost us our lives.

At the perimeter of the mounds Roger approached Elizabeth. Watching him move close to her, I surmised his intentions were less than honorable.

Roger's curious, almost obsessive, behavior toward Elizabeth made me think about a conversation I had with him back in Edinburgh after the expedition members were selected and everyone was celebrating at The King's Arms. Elizabeth was so lovely and lively that evening. Roger and I were sitting at a corner table, and he never stopped talking about how much Elizabeth admired his work and how eager she was to have him join the expedition. I was past the point of boredom and reaching the next plateau of annoyance when, after our third round, Roger confided that Elizabeth's engagement to Philip was a sham.

"What?" I was shocked. Philip had publicly announced their engagement just two weeks earlier.

"A ruse," Roger scoffed. "Philip doesna give a whit

about her. He is nothing more than an opportunist. His interest lay in capitalizing on some Evangelical group's enmity regarding evolutionary theory. Some radical clerics wish for Elizabeth's expedition tae fail, and they are willing to pay a high price for that failure."

Roger leaned close to me and whispered, "'Tis rumored that Philip is involved with one or more o the groups tae thwart the expedition."

"And what about Elizabeth?"

"Elizabeth is a brilliant, but, alas, a naïve girl. She believes Philip's lies and thinks the expedition's scientific success will bring them happiness. Ha!"

"But it can't be just the money. He would marry into Burnett's fortune. Is there something else?"

Roger got quiet. "Philip would benefit from Elizabeth's failure," he shifted his eyes from side to side, "if he could take credit for a disaster in Burnett's eyes. Then, no matter what Elizabeth's feelings may be when she returns in shame, the larger prize, Lord Monboddo's title, would be assured."

I shook my head. "Surely Elizabeth would sniff oot such a treachery."

Roger smiled. "Doesna matter. I have it on good authority the good Lord Monboddo is next to penniless, but his title opens many doors for an avaricious scoundrel like Philip. And if Philip acquired sufficient funds tae offset Burnett's economic embarrassment as well as satisfy his ego, Elizabeth would have nae power tae stop him. Unless. . .unless I could persuade her—"

Before he could finish, we were escorted to the head table for a toast.

Circumstances never allowed me to bring up the subject again, but I've often wondered about Roger's assertion, and why he told me. Could there have been some collusion between Philip and the Evangelicals that perpetrated the insurrection aboard The Cumberland? An insurrection that spiraled out of control? Roger's hope to come to Elizabeth's rescue was now meaningless, but apparently that hadn't stopped him from trying.

Roger touched Beth's shoulder.

"Ah ha!" Elizabeth pointed at an eroded space in the ground. "These are footprints."

I joined their company.

The moment he saw me, Roger withdrew from Elizabeth's side and feigned the look of a dignified colleague. "Aye, there is a trail that leads down from the north. It appears tae be a well-traveled route o some sort."

"We followed the track for some distance," I interjected. "It never faded from sight."

In the weak afternoon sunlight, we could make out the same footprints Roger and I found earlier. At this point, they fanned out from the track and circled the shell mound.

"Look here." Elizabeth squatted and pointed at what remained of a footprint of immense size, easily twice that of a normal foot. The impression sank deep into the soil and spanned across the trail, not following it.

"What ye make o it?" Roger said.

"'Tis the footprint o a giant." Elizabeth frowned in concentration. "Like the drawing in Pigafetta's journal. They have been here, gentlemen. And by the looks o things, nae that long ago."

Roger stood up and gazed in the direction of the print, toward the mountains. A pose intended to catch Elizabeth's eye, I wagered. "Would it nae be ironic if it proves tae be true? After all we have been through. Rejection by yer faither and his cohorts, the expedition's disaster. Noo tae find this. Yer theory about Magellan's giants could still be substantiated, Elizabeth. If we survive tae tell the tale."

Elizabeth looked up from studying the print. "We noo have a purpose. We must survive."

I admired Beth's courage, but I wondered if our survival was simply a matter of overcoming natural obstacles. As we walked back to the shell mounds, I made a mental note to ask Jacob what he knew about the Evangelical associations in Edinburgh.

Henry gave up his digging when the sun sank behind the mountains. He brushed off his breeches and straightened his tunic. "We are running out of daylight," he shouted. "Time we put down our toys and go home. No telling what manner of upset natives roam around here after dark." He winked at me. I didn't wink back.

Elizabeth snickered.

Roger shook his head. "Even here he is an embarrassment."

A pillar of smoke greeted us when we approached the boulders. Jacob sat near the fire holding his bloody arm, staring into the fire. "It willna stop," he muttered. "I have a confession tae make. I am a bleeder." He tried to smile. "Up to noo it did nae matter."

Elizabeth found Jacob's discarded kerchief, caked with dried blood and covered with sand. It was difficult to see closely in the weak light, but Jacob was having a difficult time staying upright. Blood was pooling at his side.

He never took his eyes off the fire. "I'm glad yer back," Jacob whispered. "Noo I'm going tae lie down for a bit." Without another word, he fell back prone on the sand and closed his eyes.

"We should nae have left him!" Elizabeth exclaimed. She grabbed the kerchief and headed toward the stream. "Do something!"

Walking behind Elizabeth, Roger spoke using an authoritarian voice, "Henry, staunch the flow until we get back. John, stoke the fire." He grabbed a battered pot Henry brought back from the tide pool. "I will fetch some water."

Henry raised his palms in frustration. "What am I supposed to use...?" He looked closely at Jacob's face. "Wake up, old man." Jacob's eyes fluttered, empty of recognition. "We're losing him," Henry said, in a matter-of-fact tone that sounded like resignation.

I felt in my pocket for the teeth I had collected at the shell mound, but there was no time to fashion them into needles, even if we had a blade. I pointed at Henry's belt. "Let me have yer belt."

"Am I the designated provider of apparel?" Henry whined.

I smiled and nodded. "Just the belt. Ye can keep the breeches. The belt is more effective than my braces."

With the belt cinched just above the wound, the flow slowed to a trickle. "We risk gangrene tae the arm by cutting off the blood supply, but at this point that seems like the lesser evil. 'Tis that or he bleeds tae death."

"True enough, Doctor Hempstead. Of course, we don't have a blade to carry out an amputation even if gangrene became an issue."

"Just so," I replied while gripping Jacob's tourniquet. I was tempted to ask Henry what he had found in his pocket this morning, but I refrained. Instead, the helpless feeling I'd felt earlier rushed over me. "We're all just waiting our turn, aren't we?"

Looking at Jacob's still form I worried that whatever secrets there may be to learn about the Evangelicals and Philip were bleeding out Jacob's arm.

After a dismal, sleepless night, a weak sun filtered through another cold blanket of morning fog. I sat, my back turned away from Jacob's still form, facing the glowing embers.

"John," Elizabeth whispered. "How is he?"

"He doesna respond, I canna feel a pulse." I didn't tell her that I had dozed off sometime during my watch and when I awoke Jacob was dead.

Elizabeth stood up and examined the corpse, then closed its lifeless eyes.

"He's gone." She was too exhausted to cry. "It's my fault."

I kept silent while Roger and Henry dragged Jacob's body away from our pitiful camp, leaving a red-tinged circle of sand behind. I wasn't of any use to anyone. I couldn't even be depended upon to keep vigil over a friend in need. By rights I should have been the casualty. How ironic it was that my years of study made not a whit of a difference in this setting. Old age and treachery be damned.

After moving Jacob, Roger came back to Elizabeth and held her hand. "Dinna fash yerself, Beth. He couldn'y been saved."

Elizabeth shook her head and removed her hand from Roger's while Henry struggled with a plank, shifting sand to hollow out a shallow grave. "I let him down," She replied. "I should have paid attention tae nursing Jacob instead o forcing him tae traverse difficult terrain. The exertion killed him." She hid her face in her hands.

Not wishing to impose myself upon Elizabeth's grief, I grabbed a stick of firewood and stumbled up to the gravesite. "Let me help." I thought maybe I could be helpful digging the graves of those put in my trust.

"Thanks," huffed Henry. "I hope Jacob doesn't mind these humble quarters."

"We might have saved him if I hadn't fallen asleep."

"Hush," Henry muttered while we scraped out the shallow trench. "Once he told us he was a bleeder, we all knew it was only a matter of time. You were the unlucky one is all."

"Thanks for that." I gave an appreciative nod. "He put his life on the line for us, ye ken that. When Peter had us all lined up in the great cabin? Jacob stood up tae him, he did. Bought us some time. Made that bastard pirate stop and consider..."

"I remember," Henry huffed, concentrating on pushing his plank deeper into the unforgiving sand. He was making a valiant effort, but his progress was minimal. My pathetic assistance made no difference.

"Ye ken what caused Peter tae take over the ship?"

"'Twas my money. As soon as he found out about it, he plotted the mutiny. Why do you ask? I thought we all knew that."

"I was just wondering if there might have been another reason, something tae do with Elizabeth's fiancé, Philip."

Elizabeth stood up. "Henry, John," she shouted. We stopped our efforts and looked back. The sun had already burned off the fog and was warming up the day. "Remove Jacob's clothing. We will need it for bandages."

Henry put his hand up to his ear. "What? Remove his clothing? Is that not some sort of sacrilege?"

"Maybe it is at Greyfriars Cemetery," Elizabeth replied, "but we are nae in Edinburgh, and nae have the luxury tae be concerned about sacrilege. Ye unnerstan? Jacob died in part because we lack bandages."

Henry and I looked at each other and considered Elizabeth's proposal. "A good idea, Beth," I shouted. "Can we leave him his undergarments?"

"Remove every stitch."

We buried Jacob just above the high-water line. Despite Elizabeth's protests, I wouldn't remove Jacob's under drawers. "Say what ye want," I replied to her complaints, "the man deserves a shred of civility."

"Tell that tae the vultures." Elizabeth pointed to the black birds circling above us.

After a hasty breakfast of water and two biscuits each, we stood silently around Jacob's grave waiting for Elizabeth to say something.

Elizabeth cleared her throat. "We have lost a dear friend, a respected colleague, and a much-needed ally. Rest ye in peace, Jacob. Please forgive us, and God help us all." She looked up from the mound of sand. "Gentlemen, we are stranded in an unsustainable environment, hundreds o uncharted miles from rescue. We have been here only two days and already our numbers have dwindled. What mishap awaits that will take the next life?" She let out a sob. "Bloody hell, I want out o this infernal sun!"

Elizabeth headed toward the stream. Above her,

their shadows cutting across the sand, the circling mass of vultures grew with every minute.

"They smell Jacob's blood," I noted. I gazed at the birds for a long moment. "Vultur gryphus. Commonly called the Andean condor, native only tae the southern Americas. I am told they can achieve a wingspan o ten feet or more. An aggressive scavenger with greatly elongated talons. God help ye if ye should accidentally fall senseless under their watchful eye. They be on ye in minutes and fighting over yer extracted, beating heart a minute after that."

"Damn it, John." Elizabeth shouted over her shoulder. "Just this once. Spare us the lecture."

As we departed the gravesite, Roger gestured for me to accompany him, and we returned to the trail we uncovered yesterday. While we were discussing the implications of the trail, Henry walked up and took a deep breath. "Beth is right, this location is unsustainable. Any suggestions?"

Roger ignored Henry and directed his reply toward me. "The question that needs asking is what do we ken? On the negative side, our food supply will soon be exhausted. We canna survive long on a few clams and the occasional fish. And Jacob taught us that one wrong move and we face dire consequences. Even were we tae be cautious, one misstep could be lethal."

I nodded and cleaned my spectacles with Roger's red-stained kerchief. "On the positive side, we have an abundant water supply and we have found evidence o habitation; civilized habitation, at that."

Henry piped in, "Do you call those rubbish piles evidence of civilization?"

"We're not talking about rubbish piles," Roger interrupted. He glared at Henry and pointed at the footprints in the sand. "John is referring tae evidence right under yer feet."

Henry scanned the impressions and made a low whistle. "Interesting. Are you sure they are not ours?"

I pointed at the naked footprints. "Are these yers?"

Roger chuckled. "Considering a winter o some rainfall and the consequential erosion o evidence, the prints canna be more than four months old. One must assume there be waystations or settlements between Buenos Aires and Puerto Santa Cruz and people be traveling there and back on a regular basis."

Henry clasped his hands in excitement. "By Jove, I venture we should follow that trail."

"Or we could wait for the travelers tae find us," I countered. "And I disagree with yer assessment o our food supply, Roger. Some foraging, perhaps at a higher elevation, will likely uncover additional sustenance."

Henry shook his head. "Waiting is rarely a successful strategy. Anyway, doing something is less boring. I would hate to die of boredom."

Roger maintained a charged silence.

"I can think o worse deaths," I muttered.

"Right," Henry went on. "I will take another look at the tide pools. It is low tide and there are still things I was unable to retrieve. Then tomorrow—"

"Nae so fast," Elizabeth interrupted from behind us. "Ye have not addressed the footprint. That o a bipedal anthropoid, twice the size o a normal human's foot."

"'Tis but a footprint," Roger replied. "But the evidence indicates the existence o something quite large. We might wish tae explore more tae the west. The print is pointing toward the mountains."

Elizabeth faced west and nodded. "I want tae pursue my search, but the truth is we canna provide proof o our own existence much less that o one or more three-hundred-pound goliaths. Still, the knowledge o their existence is heartening." She wiped her brow with a piece of Jacob's clothing. Her hair stuck to the back of her neck, and I could hear her stomach grumble. "And furthermore, I am nae going anywhere without first having a day o rest. That includes a proper bath and a full stomach of whatever ye scavengers can collect."

Beth's mention of a proper bath reminded me it was

probably the onset of her menstruation cycle. During the voyage, she had never been shy of complaining to us about its inconvenience and discomfort. I admired her open-mindedness about such things. Only a dedicated scientist could be so forthright in light of society's preponderant disapproval. That also could explain her insistence on retaining Jacob's garments.

"Agreed," Henry added before Roger could get a word in. "Since tomorrow is the Sabbath, we should observe it."

The temptation to deliver a lecture got the best of me. Remembering Elizabeth's earlier retort about my lecturing, I did my best to moderate my tone. "Pigafetta's journal noted that the giants they encountered were shy by nature, but aggressive when attacked or felt threatened. Nae amount o effort short o deadly force could stop them. I particularly remember Pigafetta's notation that the giants were intelligent. Guile was nae an effective deterrent."

I looked for acknowledgement, saw none and stumbled on. "I recommend we proceed with utmost caution and avoid direct contact at all costs. Remember, our expedition was predicated on obtaining proof o their existence, nae tae encroach upon their lives and, quite possibly, endanger ours."

Chapter Three

When the sun broke through the morning fog on our third day, our ragged group of three men and a woman stood lost in a vast, deserted landscape. Nobody moved. In front of us, a trail stretched north and south, as far as we could see.

My proposal that we take shelter and wait for rescue had fallen on deaf ears. An old man's fears of brittle bones and thin skin were brushed off by my younger colleagues as too cautious to a fault. I argued we were not outfitted for a lengthy overland walk. Our shoes were nearly threadbare, and we possessed scant protection from the unrelenting sun. We had no hat, even to share. My arguments were countered with rationalizations that lacked logic or even a practical alternative aside from the sheer joy of wanderlust. I had convinced myself to abandon their folly, but Elizabeth persuaded me to relent.

"I need ye," she had said. "Yer the only one I can trust and confide in." When I opened my mouth to protest, she shushed me. "I am also anxious about the perils that lie ahead." She took my hand. "We need yer knowledge and maturity tae overcome whatever awaits us." She dropped her voice. "Both from within as well as without, aye?" Then she smiled. "Also, ye can cook."

I chuckled, mostly to myself for giving in to Beth's flattery. Maturity indeed. What good is maturity if the mature one is a helpless impediment?

The day before, Henry had salvaged more provisions from the wreck and Elizabeth had made a crude satchel for our meager supplies using the breeks taken from our dead companion. Henry carried it over his shoulder.

"Which way should we go?" Elizabeth asked.

Nobody answered.

"It seems best that we head north, towards Buenos Aires," Roger suggested. "Since Buenos Aires is a busy commercial center, we stand a better chance o encountering a ship – or caravan, perhaps – by heading in that direction." He gave us a condescending nod, looked northward and waited for everyone to congratulate him on his brilliant suggestion.

"I propose we travel south," Henry countered.

I swear I could see the hair on the back of Roger's neck stand up.

"And why is that?" I interrupted before Roger could reply in order to avoid a shouting match. "'Tis the south-bound direction shorter?"

"No. The miles make no difference either way. It just seems to me that traveling southward feels like going downhill. One always travels up when heading north and down when traveling south, yes? For example, one never travels 'up' to London, unless you're coming from Brighton. But, heaven knows, nobody goes to Brighton anymore...."

Elizabeth tried in vain to stop giggling and I broke into a grin.

"That is the most ridiculous thing I have ever heard!" Roger shouted. "I am a scientist. I do *nae* have tae listen tae such gibberish when we are making a decision as important as this."

"I doubt he meant it seriously," Elizabeth said. "Aye, Henry?"

"Well, it may sound foolish, but—"

"Ye be the epitome of foolishness." Roger gave in to his simmering resentment and he marched up to Henry, stiff as a popinjay.

I thought Roger's overreaction was just as comical as Henry's proposal.

"I have suffered long enough listening tae yer asinine opinions and bad judgment!"

Henry stood his ground and shoved one fist into his pocket.

Aha. I remembered the last time he explored that pocket. I took it to be a weapon of some sort. A blade, maybe. Something he didn't want us to know about.

"That was uncalled for," Henry replied. "It was an opinion only. I demand an apology this instant."

"Gentlemen, please." Worried about the secret weapon, I screwed up my courage and stood between the two men as I had watched Elizabeth do two days earlier, much to my discredit. The prospect of watching broken bones and gouged eyes atrophy in this unforgiving country was too horrible a prospect to allow, even at the cost of being injured myself. "We will nae find any solutions coming from yer squabbling. It is appropriate that we leave the choice of direction to our leader." I took a cautious step back. "Beth, which way should we go?"

Roger unclenched his fists. Henry removed his hand from his pocket.

"I willna say anything until ye both shake hands,"

Elizabeth said.

The two men continued glaring at each other until Henry stuck out his hand. After much huffing and puffing, Roger reciprocated then quickly withdrew.

"As for the direction, I studied the direction o the footprints at the shell mound, and 'tis clear that the majority point south. I suggest we do likewise on the assumption that the preponderance o south-bound traffic in the recent past indicates an interim destination, such as a waystation, is nearby."

Elizabeth waited for a reaction, but it seemed her position, as well as her logic, ended the controversy. Roger nodded in agreement. Henry and I did the same.

Without another word, we began walking in single file. Henry took the lead, followed by Roger. Elizabeth and I brought up the rear of our desperate expedition in search of rescue. We followed a track we hoped would take us to the little provisioning settlement of Puerto Santa Cruz, approximately seven hundred unexplored miles away, and from there back to Scotland.

The first things we discovered along the trail were bunions, blisters, insect bites and aching muscles. Even our two able-bodied champions were not immune to these discomforts. What worried me was these hardships occurred while we walked on level ground under favorable weather; hot in the afternoon, perhaps, but favorable considering the alternatives.

It quickly became apparent Roger and Henry outpaced Elizabeth and myself by a significant margin, separating our expedition into two distant pairs. I shouted when the two Olympians vanished ahead of us, but I was either unheard or ignored. Not long afterward, Elizabeth stopped, leaned into the shadow of a rocky outcrop, and wiped her brow. "Save yer breath," she said. "We are nae competitors in their ego-fueled race." I complied by sitting at her feet and giving my ankle a rest. "We canna be a unified group until one o them suffers a mishap," Beth added.

"Or one mishaps the other," I quipped, allowing us both a chuckle.

"Either way," Elizabeth concluded with a frown, "mark my words, it willna be long before we have more problems tae deal with."

The four of us had agreed to a midday rest stop, and when Elizabeth and I caught up with our partners, they were resting in a clearing beside the trail. We were relieved to find them peacefully minding themselves. They sat some distance from each other on a patch of grasses surrounded by a variety of shrubs, some of which looked to be related to the fuchsia.

Henry got to his feet and waved a cheery hello when

we arrived. Roger, sitting cross-legged with both his hands near his face, ignored us. "I was about to retrace my steps," Henry said. "It appears our pace led us farther down the trail than I expected."

I found myself a comfortable tuft of grass and lowered my weary backside to rest, accompanied by a groan. "I daresay ye both left us in yer dust."

Sadly, my rest was short lived. Elizabeth shamed me into activity whilst she busied herself portioning out our lunch ration, so I reluctantly got up and investigated the flora that surrounded the clearing. Despite my discomfort, the effort proved to be beneficial. I was particularly interested in finding edible roots or tubers, but my attention was drawn to an abundance of berries, some black and blue, others a striking red color. I took the chance they were not poisonous or otherwise disagreeable and bit off a tiny portion. They seemed to be palatable enough to chew and swallow without ill effect, so I picked enough to experiment with later. A mash, perhaps? Or a tea? I also was interested in the reddish fruit from a thorny succulent bush that tasted quite refreshing.

All the while Roger was absorbed in something I couldn't see, something he carefully cradled in his hands, staring with rapt attention. I was tempted to ask him what was so interesting, but Elizabeth saved me.

"'Tis nae much," she said, handing me two pieces of hardtack and half a biscuit. "We don't know when we will be re-provisioned, so I be keeping our shares as minimal as possible." While she handed Henry his portion, she scanned the line of shrubs. "Is there water nearby?"

Henry shook his head. "We must be between water courses. They seem to be spaced a couple miles apart, but there's no guarantee any are running. I decided to stop here and forego a longer stretch on the pretext we'd prefer rest to refreshment."

Roger lifted his head and spat. "Ye decided wrong, o course. Hydration is far more important than rest." He dropped whatever was in his hands and took Elizabeth's proffered food without comment. Elizabeth jumped back, an alarmed look on her face, and movement near Roger's leg caught my eye when he let go of his object of interest. Twigs and grass stalks shifted about while something scurried into the wall of shrubs.

My curiosity got the better of me. "What was that ye be handling?"

"A scorpion," Roger answered. "It stung me on the leg when we first arrived. It apparently lost its stinger after the strike."

"A scorpion? Good Lord, man!" I got up. "Let me see—"

Roger snarled at me. "Leave me be," he grumbled. "I be taking care o myself."

I hadn't any knowledge about scorpions. The little information I have heard from colleagues in Spain and Italy was the European scorpion's venom was not deadly in most cases. However, depending on the victim, it could cause side effects, some dangerous. The problem was we had no idea what to expect from a South American scorpion's venom. I proposed applying a poultice, but Roger would have none of it.

Elizabeth sat quietly until Roger finished his food. "Can ye stand and walk?" she asked when he swallowed his last morsel.

Roger touched his leg and smiled. "It'll take more than a scorpion tae finish me off." He sat up and cleared his throat. "More tae the point, I'm considering this minor mishap tae be an opportunity for scientific observation. We know the scorpions that inhabit the higher latitudes, such as Spain and Portugal, are relatively benign. Whereas their Asian and desert cousins are much more venomous." He rubbed his lower leg where red swelling appeared through a tear in his stocking. "Since we're at the latitudinal antipodes from southern Europe, I'm interested tae find if these scorpions have a similar sting."

He slowly got his feet under him. Then, with

46

deliberate effort, he stood. His smile became forced, he clinched his jaw as he took an unsteady step. "There is some discomfort," he admitted, holding his leg. "I need tae walk off the pain." Two steps later he dropped to his knees and Elizabeth rushed to him. "Och, Roger!" she cried. She held his head and pointed at Henry. "Quick, get me some —" Before she finished, Roger went limp in her arms.

"Keep his chest elevated," I said. "Keep the venom from entering his heart." I sprinkled the last of my water on my kerchief and wiped Roger's brow. He was hot to the touch. "Hurry, Henry," I finished Elizabeth's plea. "Take what containers ye can and bring us some water." I answered Henry's perplexed look with a sharp retort. "I care nae where ye go. Just find water."

"Och Roger, ye be such a silly fool," Elizabeth muttered, staring at Roger's red face. His breathing was rapid and shallow. "Tell me he willna die, John. Please."

Roger's pulse was racing when I placed my fingers against his wrist. His skin was flushed and felt damp. All I could do was attempt to cool his brow. I told Elizabeth to busy herself preparing a place for Roger. "We'll stay here for the night," I said. "Make him comfortable." I was not in a frame of mind to make false promises.

Henry surprised me by returning sooner than I expected carrying a tin full of water in each hand. "A brook crosses the trail not more than twenty yards ahead," he said. "Damnedest thing, I nearly fell in while scanning the horizon for signs of water." He handed one tin to Elizabeth and looked for a long moment at Roger. "His reaction to the sting is peculiar...." He lifted Roger's right eyelid, then the other. "His pupils are dilated."

I nodded. "I read an English translation of a treatise by Henri-François LeDran about a condition associated with gunshot wounds that translates tae shock." The prospect of another burial disturbed me, but I tried to remain calm. "Roger's condition seems tae be similar from what I remember."

Elizabeth tilted Roger's head back and carefully put the tin to his lips. As the liquid trickled down his throat, Roger jerked his head away and coughed. A long moan later, he opened his eyes and growled. "What in God's name...?" When he focused on Elizabeth's distressed face, he struggled to sit up. Elizabeth helped him. "Ye fainted, Roger. The scorpion, it made ye ill."

Roger took the tin from Elizabeth's hand and drank. "Unfortunate turn o events," he said after two hasty gulps. "Seems the experiment is inconclusive." He looked at Henry and me. "Shall we continue? We still have a few hours o daylight left." He leaned forward, struggling to stand, but wound up on his knees. "Give me a moment," he said. "Tae get my strength back."

"We are nae going anywhere," I told him.

That evening around a low fire was a quiet affair, all of us too exhausted to come up with entertainment or even light conversation. After our meal, I offered up a handful of berries. "These are plentiful and are digestible, at least in wee portions." Everyone took a sample. "I hope tae experiment cooking with them as a mash when the opportunity allows." Nobody objected.

I watched Roger as long as I could during the night, and he slept peacefully until my eyes could no longer stay open. As I drifted off, I hoped I wouldn't find another corpse in the morning.

After struggling with a slow start, Roger resumed walking the following day without complaint. Elizabeth and I drew a sigh of relief. I was skeptical Roger was fully recovered and considered another day of recuperation the better option. *What was the rush*? I asked myself. But I avoided the subject to keep the peace.

A clanging noise interrupted my thoughts at midday as I limped along the trail, favoring my right ankle. My mind was a thousand miles away, at St Andrews. I was recalling when a friend, Brian, had handed me a package, wrapped in a red ribbon, as a birthday gift. I smiled as I recalled having hugged Brian. "Happy birthday," he had said. "And many happy returns o the day." It was nothing, really, but I was touched.

The clang happened again, dragging my attention back to the trail. I stopped, listened, and scanned the terrain. Dark clouds covered the mountain peaks to the west. "Did anyone hear something?" Nobody answered. I turned around and discovered that my only companions were the condors circling in broad arcs overhead. "Hello!" I hollered.

The clang happened again. "What the bloody hell?" Looking down, I spotted three tins on the trail behind me. Another one glinted in the sunlight farther back. It had been my turn to carry the satchel and it was splitting at the seams. Wisps of fog blew in from the sea, but the horizon still shimmered in the midday heat. The landscape was changing. I could see trees in the distance and, closer, the ground gave way to more vegetation.

I felt exposed. "Hello!" I cupped my hands around my mouth and shouted again, but there was no reply. After collecting the lost tins and tying up Elizabeth's pack as best I could, I picked up my pace.

From behind dense brush, a group of onlookers watched John collect the items he had dropped, the ocean breeze carrying his scent to them. "This one has separated himself from the great warrior," one noted. "He can be eliminated as it should be." Another member with graying hair and eyes that were not as clear as the others held up his hand. "He will take us to the others." The one who spoke first lowered his eyes and fell silent.

When I caught up with Elizabeth, she was hobbling almost as badly as I was. Upon closer inspection, her shoes were coming apart, just as I anticipated, no doubt from exposure to seawater and the strain of sustained marching. Walking over uneven ground wasn't helping my ankle, either. It was most painful. "I must stop a moment," I pleaded. Elizabeth paused and I found an uncomfortable place to sit on a hot boulder with no protection from the sun. Henry and Roger were nowhere to be seen.

I held out the damaged satchel and pointed to the rents in the fabric. "Yer excellent satchel is, sadly, nae match for our tins' punishing weight and ceaseless jostling. I may have lost a tin or two along the trail before I made the discovery."

Elizabeth gave the satchel a cursory inspection then handed it back. "There's nae we can do until we find a place that allows me tae make repairs." She wiped her brow with her forearm and avoided my eyes. "Sorry, John."

Roger appeared, much to our surprise, seemingly from out of nowhere. He approached us, favoring his injured leg. "Did I hear ye say something about lost provisions?" He eyed me with a most unfriendly grimace.

I nodded. "I canna be sure, but there's a chance some tins—"

"Ye bloody well better trot back tae be sure, should ye nae?!"

I swallowed the urge to answer back with an uncivil rejoinder, assuring myself instead, Roger's attitude indicated he was returning to his curmudgeonly self. "I'm resting my injured ankle," I replied. "If ye be keen on investigating forthwith, and yer leg can handle it, I suggest ye make a reconnaissance yerself." I pointed to his injured leg. "Is yer leg getting better?"

Roger rubbed the area where he was stung and winced. "My leg is nane o yer business, sir. Yer business is tae retrieve the supplies ye lost due tae negligence."

Elizabeth sighed and sat next to me. "Enough, Roger. The point is nane o us are wont to do any more walking than we must." She examined what was left of a shoe heel. "These willna last much longer." She kicked off her other shoe in frustration.

"People walk this trail barefoot," Roger interjected.

Elizabeth stared at him and chuckled. "Be ye volunteering?"

"I am most certainly nae." Roger huffed. He rubbed

his sore leg again. "'Tis merely an observation regarding our options when we inevitability get down tae three pair o shoes for eight feet. We may have tae alternate."

I looked at Elizabeth and she returned my glance with a bemused smile. "I would prefer a gig," she said.

"Or a comfortable sedan chair," I added. "Roger could provide ample locomotion."

Roger's face turned redder than it already was. "Ye mock me!" He stammered. "I willna stand for ... for this ... this insolence!" He took one step toward me and grabbed his hurt leg. With a groan, the leg gave way and he collapsed.

Roger's breathing became shallow gasps. I removed his stocking to discover the swelling and discoloration around the area where he had been stung was worse than I thought. He didn't resist my investigation. "The poison is nae through with him yet," I said.

Elizabeth nodded. "We worsened his condition with our jesting. He's so sensitive and short tempered. He succumbs tae emotional strain faster than physical exertion."

"What in God's name?" Henry appeared and stared at our companion. "Is he badly injured?"

Elizabeth shrugged. "We're nae sure. It seems the scorpion sting is still affecting him."

For a quiet moment, the three of us considered the possibility of a new alignment in our group if Roger became a liability. It would leave it to the three of us to make a go of it.

Another groan from Roger broke the quiet. He twisted his head around, squinting in the sun, to look at us. When he caught sight of Elizabeth, he grimaced but said nothing. The harsh sunlight picked up every pore and every whisker.

Elizabeth squatted and wrapped a wet strip of Jacob's clothing around Roger's inflamed leg. "Where did ye go?" she said.

Henry scanned the horizon. "Roger disappeared and I found myself alone some ways down the trail. Funny thing about it, as I made my way back looking for you, it felt like something, or someone, was stalking me."

"How so?" I asked, following his gaze.

"Nothing I could see; a high whistle 'tis all. Not quite a bird sound, almost out of range of my hearing. Whenever I looked in the direction of the sound, I detected movement, a shadow flitting between boulders. I suppose it could have been my imagination."

We all looked and listened until Roger uttered another groan.

"Water," he uttered.

While Elizabeth tended to Roger, I lowered my

voice. "I fear we need tae reconsider our strategy. For one thing, Beth and I won't last much longer at this pace. And for another—"

"Later," Henry interjected. "We need to get on our way." He paid no attention to me.

Beth and I propped Roger up to a sitting position. He kept silent, his eyes downcast in defeat, with not a hint of defiance.

As we got our things together, Roger spoke. "Help me up."

Elizabeth ignored him, but I helped him to his feet.

Roger leaned on me for support, but he managed to move. We made a slow but successful practice walk. "Does it hurt? I asked when we stopped.

After a deep breath, Roger returned an almost imperceptible nod. "I'll take a ride on that gig," he smiled.

I smiled back. "Buck up," I said. "Humor is a sure sign of improvement."

"There is water and shelter a short distance ahead," Henry said, looking in the direction from whence he came.

I looked for moving shadows while I wrapped my ankle as tight as I could endure. "Just how short a distance?"

"It hardly matters, does it? We should get there –

soon." A peal of thunder coming from the dark clouds building above the western mountains punctuated the urgent tone in Henry's voice.

"I wish tae know only tae assure my tormented ankle that today's ordeal will be soon over."

Elizabeth took hold of my free arm. "John and I will help each other," she said to Henry. "Assist Roger, if ye please."

"Huzzah!" I exclaimed when we saw evidence of an encampment as we approached a stream. Elizabeth had found me a stick with sufficient strength to keep some of the weight off my ankle, but it was hard to handle over rough terrain. "Just as I thought. Our fellow travelers use rest stations. I wager we'll find them at regular intervals." I patted Elizabeth on the shoulder as she helped me cross a rocky patch.

"Don't be so sure," she chuckled. "They may be irregular intervals for some of us."

I winced more than nodded to acknowledge Beth's comment. My ankle throbbed.

When we reached the treeline, a lean-to shelter welcomed us along with tobacco shards and a bottle, corked and half full of rum. Wood shavings and bones lay about a cleared camping area.

That night, rain squalls raced overhead, pushed along by strong westerly winds. Inside, Henry, Beth and

I sat around a low fire and drank the rum. Roger kept to himself, huddled in a corner. After having performed another taste test and finding the berries palatable, I had prepared a mash consisting of berries and some tubers I dug up before the rain started. It wasn't haggis, but with the help of the rum, it supplemented the few provisions we had left from the boat. I approached Roger, offering him a share of our dinner and some drink, but he wouldn't let me come near.

"I hope he benefits from a night's sleep," I said, handing Elizabeth the bottle. "His reaction is so severe I'm worried for his life."

Henry stared into the coals. "Or worse," he said. "He becomes so disabled he can't walk."

I examined my bandaged ankle. "I may be near that point already."

Elizabeth held her damaged shoe to the light of the fire. "We'll stay here tomorrow. My shoe and the satchel need attention before we can resume our march. The rest will do all o us some good." She looked at Roger's quiet corner. "And if Roger doesn't improve, we will make another plan."

Henry smiled and continued watching the coals. "Like waiting for company to arrive?"

"Correct. We would need tae make preparations for such an encounter." She stared into the darkness. "We might get company sooner than we expect."

Maybe it was the rum, but in the ensuing quiet, I found myself reflecting on the earlier conversation I had with Roger about Elizabeth's betrothed, Philip. I wondered if Elizabeth had even a whisper of a doubt. Summoning my liquid courage, I cleared my throat with a nervous cough. "Has Roger ever talked tae ye about Philip?"

Elizabeth perked up. "Philip? Pray tell, what do ye mean?"

Henry gave me a look of surprise but kept quiet. I felt a shiver of anxiety for having brought up the subject, especially seeing Elizabeth look at me so intently, but I was committed. I hoped I wouldn't wind up lying next to Roger with wounds of my own. "Roger once told me, and mind ye, this was after a few pints, that he thought Philip was a fraud."

"A fraud?"

"Aye. He said Philip had nae sincere feelings towards ye and was solely interested in profiting from the expedition's failure."

"Why, that's preposterous! Where did he get such an idea?"

"He'd heard a rumor that Philip was carrying out a plan formulated by a group of hardline Evangelicals who wished tae thwart the expedition's success. At the expense of yer feelings, I'm sad tae say."

Elizabeth gasped and put her hand to her bosom. "I trust Philip with all my heart. How could that possibly be?"

"I know, Elizabeth. That is the question, is it nae?"

A rustling noise came from outside our camp. Elizabeth and I both turned to investigate but saw nothing.

Henry put his hand in his pocket.

The group of three observers sat silently, oblivious to the weather, watching the campsite. "The signs are clear, Gilgamesh returns," the oldest observer remarked. This observer was a massive creature, over seven feet tall, his hair streaked with gray, tattered mats of fur hung from his back and flanks indicating countless battles won and lost. "His hair is the color of blood as the prophecy foretold."

Another observer spoke. "He reeks of bloody combat."

The eldest pointed to the young one, "Watch over him until we return."

After the storm blew out, I freed myself from the tangle of legs and arms and hobbled outside. It was dark, but a new moon blinked in between clouds. The wind chilled me, and I hurried out as best I could, away from the lean-to, looking for a place to relieve myself. I might have waited until dawn, but an old man's fear of incontinence spirited me on.

The wet vegetation slapped against my face and the muddy ground made my errand even more uncomfortable. Guided by the moon's feeble light, I found an open space and squatted. It was slow going. As I struggled with my wretched bowels, I heard a high-pitched whistle, similar to what Henry described the day before. "Go away!" I barked, trying to sound more annoyed than afraid. In response, the shrubs in front of me began to shake.

The excitement opened the flood gates, as It were, and when I was done, I stood up and rallied my courage. "Who goes there?"

"'Tis only I," Henry announced, stepping through the shrubbery. "I wondered where you had gone. Whew! You could have gone a bit farther, mind you."

"The hell ye say," I griped, hiking up my breeks. "Ye have frightened an old man. Was that yer whistling?"

Henry shook his head. "I heard whistling as well. Woke me up. It came from around here somewhere."

It was just turning light, and I could see columns of mist rising from the saturated vegetation. "Could ye detect movement?"

Henry shook his head. "Your shouting distracted me. I thought maybI.."

Elizabeth appeared behind Henry. "What is all the bellowing about? And what is that I smell?"

"Well, excuse me," I railed.

"'Tis nae that." Elizabeth pressed her face against wet leaves and branches, breathing in. "Something else. Like a wet dog. Very strong over here."

The wet foliage captured a strong scent of musk. So strong, even the weak human sense of smell could detect it.

"Fascinating. It appears something is tracking us." Elizabeth followed the scent trail until it died out in an open space. "I want the both of ye tae urinate along this pathway. We should introduce ourselves."

Henry sniggered. "Maybe we should beat on our chests as well."

"Nae a bad idea, Henry. That will give whatever it is a laugh if they are nae laughing already."

Henry imitated the stylized gorilla sounds and movements we'd all seen at exhibitions of curiosities up and down Edinburgh's High Street. Elizabeth recoiled at first, then joined in the merriment. It was a release of tension, maybe at Henry's expense, but he didn't mind. We were still civilized enough to laugh.

"A braw performance, lad," I exclaimed.

Henry took a bow. "And now, for his next act, Henry the Great will crawl on his belly–"

Elizabeth shushed Henry and began making her way back to the lean-to. "Gentlemen, please," she said with a touch of sarcasm, "do as ye be told."

Chapter Four

When we returned to the lean-to, Roger moved outside and sat in a ray of sun. The swelling under his stocking had not subsided and the look on his face indicated it was still painful. He paid no attention to us while I prepared a breakfast of hardtack wrapped in green leaves that looked and tasted remarkably like lettuce. He ignored his portion when I placed it in front of him and sat silently, eyes downcast. I felt sorry for him even though his attitude was getting more and more difficult.

Henry and Elizabeth left him alone.

After gulping down my meager ration, I tried to get my mind off hunger by tending to my ankle and talking about what lay ahead. "Building on what Elizabeth said yesterday about reconsidering our strategy," I pointed to Elizabeth's crude shoe repair work, "I dinnae think moving as a group is the best plan of action." I looked at Henry. "Assuming he recovers, ye and Roger be better suited for rapid travel. Elizabeth and I be less so."

When I rolled down my stocking to take a peek this morning, I noticed my ankle had turned a nasty-looking tinge of yellow during the night and the swelling had not subsided. "Instead, I propose ye both scout ahead tae find the next camp. Elizabeth and I will follow as best we can at our own speed."

Roger continued staring at the ground, not saying a word. I couldn't tell if he was listening or not.

"We have tae assume the rest points will continue some distance apart. Ye both should be able tae find the easiest possible route in half the time. Then, while one o ye makes camp, the other can come back tae assist us. O course, if Roger canna walk, we should remain here and wait until help arrives."

Roger looked up. "I can walk." He shifted his position and sat up. "Yer plan doubles the time it takes tae cover the distance."

"Nobody said anything about time," Elizabeth stopped her repair work and dropped her shoe. "Chances are good our destiny will be a string o shallow graves along this God-forsaken path. Nae one will care how long it takes us tae get there."

Roger took a deep breath and slowly exhaled. "We must push on tae Puerto Santa Cruz with utmost haste before we are given up for dead." With a grimace, Roger struggled to his feet. "I can walk," he repeated. "Alone, I'll get there in half the time. Then I will organize a rescue party."

"What makes ye so sure ye can organize a rescue?" I eyed Roger's hardtack, angry to see it wasted among ants and beetles. Roger's assumption prompted me to explore the conspiracy theory he had told me about earlier.

Roger hesitated. "I am certain o that." He took a quick look at Elizabeth. "Before we left, I promised yer faither tae keep ye out of harm's way. In return, he promised tae send a supply ship tae supplement our provisions or bring us home if need be. The plan was tae rendezvous with our expedition at Puerto Santa Cruz in three months' time. If we were nae there, they would sell the supplies tae the villagers and depart before the onset o winter."

In the ensuing silence, Roger cleared his throat. "He made me promise nae tae divulge his plan."

Elizabeth glared back at Roger. "I dinnae believe a word o it. Ye be telling these lies about my faither and about Philip tae mock me."

Indeed, the idea seemed far-fetched. Roger himself had told me that Lord Monboddo hardly possessed the fiscal means to maintain his household, much less hire and provision a ship suitable to make an eight-thousand league voyage. It seemed unlikely Henry's financial associates would add to their already considerable investment. Lord Monboddo had made it clear he wanted nothing to do with Henry's people.

"An interesting postulation, Roger," I replied. "And how did Lord Monboddo plan tae finance such a venture?"

"I wasna given any o his plan's details, only his promise tae carry it out."

"Hogwash!" Elizabeth shouted at Roger. "Mark my words, gentlemen. If we succeed in leaving this remote shore, it will nae be on account o any heroics on my faither's part."

"I want very much tae prove ye be wrong." Roger gave Elizabeth a quick bow. "I am wasting time here," he said and hobbled away from the campsite.

I fully expected him to stop at any moment and laugh for having surprised us. Was he truly heading off? Before I could think otherwise, Henry bolted, tackled our crazed colleague from behind and wrestled him to the ground. The scuffle lasted but a minute.

Lying on top of him, Henry shouted over Roger's oaths. "I will accompany you, Roger," he said.

When Henry released him, Roger sat up, rubbing his leg. "I have lost yer trust," he said. "Let me make this wee sacrifice in hopes I may be able tae save our lives." Grabbing Henry's proffered hand, Roger got back on his feet. He didn't refuse Henry's offer, instead, he resumed a slow, unsteady walk without another word.

Henry directed a sly wink toward us. "Go ahead then," he said. "Let me gather a few things and catch up with you."

Elizabeth buried her head in her hands. "Och noo we've lost another life."

"He's not lost quite yet," Henry said. "Let me entertain him for as long as he lasts. The exercise might clear his head. I'll come back to fetch you to wherever we wind up."

"By the by, Henry," I replied. "Ask Roger if he knows anything about Lord Monboddo's relations with Philip."

Elizabeth gasped. "John, I dinnae believe yer story. Ye canna possibly think my faither had conspired with Philip tae thwart the expedition."

"Nae, I do nae insinuate that Lord Monboddo wished us harm. But would nae yer faither have preferred for our expedition tae return empty-handed?

67

'Tis conceivable yer faither, with Philip's assistance, might have planted the hope o rescue in Roger's head tae disrupt our investigations, plant a seed o discord, ye might say." I laughed at the irony of my supposition. "Ha! Little did he ken—"

Elizabeth made her hands into fists; she leaned forward, her face inches from mine. "How dare ye say such a thing! Faither was unhappy with my plans, true enough. But he would never...."

Henry interjected before Elizabeth could continue. "I will pose the question, John, but I doubt much will come of it. A preposterous idea, what?" With a nod to me, he held out his hand toward Elizabeth.

"Och, Henry." Elizabeth clutched Henry's hand and held it for a long moment.

I kept my mouth shut for a change.

"I hope tae God, I see ye, and ... and Roger soon," Elizabeth murmured as Henry pried himself loose and turned away.

After Henry left, Elizabeth made a point of ignoring me and busied herself with repairing her shoe and the satchel as best she could.

I took my punishment as best I could by brewing another cup of dandelion tea and gagging it down while investigating succulents growing in a quiet place next to the stream. The wild card, of course, was Peter, the first mate turned pirate. I doubted anyone wished to see us killed, or the next closest thing ... except Peter. He must have decided on his own to take Henry's money and run instead of returning to Scotland for whatever modest remittance Lord Monboddo could muster. And if he never showed up at Edinburgh, how long will Monboddo wait?

I was relieved to see Henry and Roger leave. I hadn't felt well since the incident this morning, and the acrimony wasn't helping. Elizabeth ignored my muted sighs and groans until nightfall. While we listened to the crackling campfire, she asked me how I was feeling.

I knew she really wanted to question me more about her faither, but I evaded the subject by waxing on about my condition. "'Tis hard tae identify," I said after finishing another wild dandelion tea. "Nae only my ankle, more just a general weariness. Nae strength and very little enthusiasm. My arm starts tae hurt noo and again. Getting older, I guess." I leaned back against a rock and tried to get comfortable. The dying fire whispered a lullaby.

"Ye canna sleep yet." Elizabeth slapped my ankle with a stick.

"Ach! That's my sore ankle!" I whined. There was no use pretending to be asleep.

Elizabeth cocked her head, leaned forward, and peered at me through the smoke. "Do ye think my faither and Philip are responsible for the insurrection? Is that what ye be saying?"

I knew it would come to this. "Forgive me," I whined some more and rubbed my ankle. "Only an old man's paranoia." I hoped that would satisfy her, but she waited expectantly for me to drop the other shoe, so to speak. "It's nae secret that yer faither was less than enthusiastic about the expedition. And if Philip was indeed conspiring with an Evangelical group of dissenters tae thwart the expedition, then the two had something in common, did they not?"

I expected Elizabeth to throw a rock at me, but instead, she leaned back and smiled at the heavens. "What if it were true?" I continued. "What if Peter and his men were instructed tae somehow interfere with the expedition's progress, but the plan went awry?"

"Awry? How do ye ken?"

"Henry's money. Once Peter found out about Henry's money, he might have decided tae thumb his nose at all parties concerned, take the bounty, and go rogue. 'Twas a considerable sum, was it nae? Plus, the ship thrown in for good measure."

Elizabeth's eyes were lost in shadows from the firelight that danced around our campsite. She nodded and laughed. "Too many things," she said out loud.

I laughed with her. We laughed at the folly of being stranded and lost yet still worrying about things beyond our control.

"What I would nae do for my pipe and a spot o sherry." I felt a tingling sensation in my left arm and ignored it by talking. "The King's Arms always had the best sherry. And cheese and brandy. We all loved their brandy. And it was there that yer faither proposed a theory about the common origins o human evolutionary development based on the universal myth o giants. I think the brandy helped."

Elizabeth had a dreamy smile on her face. "Remember how enthusiastic he was?"

"I remember when Boswell read from Pigafetta's log, where it mentions giants, I was struck by how similar his descriptions were with the epic tales o giants both in the new world and the old. The Cherufe in the Mapuche culture and Gilgamesh in Mesopotamia, for example. I told ye I thought Pigafetta's giants, real or imagined, were related in some way. They could be a living relic o an ancient oral tradition, known the world over." My ankle gave a twinge. "Was yer decision tae search for the giants motivated by family rivalry?"

Elizabeth was slow to respond. "I had tae find out, John. 'Twas the size o the bones that were brought back from Magellan's expedition that intrigued me. Nae Pigafetta's notes. Nae entirely, anyway. Based on the length o the tibia, the animal had tae be at least seven feet tall."

"Maybe yer faither couldn't bear the idea of sharing...." My stomach rumbled and demanded attention. "Excuse me," I interjected before I could finish my thought. "I must take care o a call o nature."

"Be ye well?" Elizabeth helped me as I struggled to get up.

"I feel a wee bit nauseous." I managed to smile, "I wager 'tis the brandy."

For three days Elizabeth and I tended to tasks, trying not to count the passage of time. From dawn to dusk Beth did the best she could to finish mending the satchel and repairing our shoes while I foraged and cooked – or I should say, experimented with cooking – native plants. Beth was my patient and forgiving participant. The tubers were my most significant success, best boiled and mashed. Although the juicy red fruit I had found earlier was plentiful and easy to harvest, we agreed that the berries lacked flavor no matter how I prepared them. Still, they were a welcome treat. Sadly, neither of us had the skill or stomach to hunt for meat. Nights were quiet affairs, next to the fire, drinking my exotic tea and listening for Henry until we dropped off to sleep.

A dull light broke through high clouds on the morning of the fourth day, painting shadows across the camp's open space. Elizabeth sat nearby, humming a tune while working on her shoes. The wind was coming from the west, from the mountains. Clouds swirled around the highest peaks.

I had finished my morning ablution and was putting on my spectacles when Henry's voice startled me. "Elizabeth, 'tis me, Henry."

"Henry!" Elizabeth jumped up. "We've been so worried. Where's Roger?"

I saw bloodstains on Henry's tunic. "What in heaven's name?" I peered at Henry, cocked my head, and waited for the worst.

Henry avoided looking back at me. "Dead; murdered, really. Something or someone deliberately killed him. I saw it happen. The incident was meant to kill us both." Besides the blood, his tunic and breeks were filthy and torn in places. His hands and arms were covered with scratches, and his face haggard, like he'd been through a terrible ordeal.

Elizabeth's hands flew to her throat and she gasped. "Someone or *something*? What happened?"

I tried not to look skeptical, but I figured next he would tell us a giant ape was the culprit. "Come sit down," I offered. "I'll fix us a spot o tea. Would ye like tae wash up a bit first?"

Henry nodded and excused himself. When he returned from the stream, I handed him a steaming tin of my favorite blueberry tea. Elizabeth led him to our fire pit and after we were seated, she put her hand on his. "Tell us what happened, Henry."

Henry took a sip and sat quietly for a minute. "We were heading down a steep grade toward a river bottom. We both were excited to discover the river and eager to investigate." Henry hesitated. "A little too eager, perhaps. Roger was ahead of me when a large boulder, sitting on the edge of an outcropping above the trail, suddenly shifted. Two figures were standing behind the boulder. I swear, they pushed it off the ledge ... and it struck Roger."

"A boulder?" Elizabeth shook her head in disbelief. "Och my God, Henry. Where is he now?"

"I dragged him down to the river and buried him in a sandbar. It was the only thing I could do."

Henry might have been telling the truth, but I needed more material to fill the holes in his story. "Start from the beginning," I said.

Henry looked at Elizabeth and sighed. "We were walking amiably enough, and I told Roger about my experiences while serving as a supply officer with the

Bombay Army in India. Just to make conversation."

"Aye. Go on."

"Well, he seemed interested, so I explained about collecting Indian antiquities and shipping them to England for sale."

"Why was Roger interested?" I asked.

"Because he asked me if that was where I got the money to invest in the expedition."

I was tempted to hear more on that subject myself, but now was not the time. "I'd like tae hear more about that, but let's get back tae the events that led tae Roger's death."

"Right." Henry gave me a nod and a serious frown. "As we continued along the trail, I realized it would be too steep for you and Elizabeth, so I retraced my steps until I came to a patch of disturbed ground I hadn't noticed before. A turn in the trail had been intentionally hidden. The trail we had followed led in the same direction, but along a steeper incline. Whereas the hidden trail was a gentler slope." He took another sip of tea. "The work was hardly noticeable when I first passed the site, heading downhill, but it was quite apparent when climbing back."

"Intentionally, ye say." This seemed fanciful to me. Who or what would go tae so much trouble? "And how came ye tae that conclusion?"

"There was cut brush laid over the original trail and a new trail had been cleared. When I shouted for Roger to come see, that's when he walked into the trap."

"Ye refer tae the boulder ye mentioned earlier?"

"Aye. I cried out for him to stop, but 'twas too late. The boulder hit him full in the face and chest. It carried him down the canyon and he disappeared into dense brush."

"What about the two figures?"

"They also disappeared."

Sitting behind a wall of brush, a half-mile away, the onlookers shifted their weight and the eldest one raised his eyebrows. Disappointment emanated from his gray eyes, casting an uneasy mood among the rest.

"Gilgamesh must reach the Temple alone," a second observer whispered.

"He must cleanse the temple and dwell there alone," the eldest confirmed, stroking his chin. "As the prophecy foretold."

The two young ones waited for their punishment; their eyes cast downward in shame.

"You have failed my trust," the eldest hissed. He gestured at the second observer. "Take them away."

After another sip of tea and a bite of hardtack, Henry

continued. "It took me the rest of the day to find Roger. The boulder had propelled him down the incline and drove him into a wall of thorny branches. His head looked like it had gone seven rounds with a prize fighter, but 'twas intact. His right arm was bent unnaturally behind him, and a deep gash exposed boney parts of his right leg."

Elizabeth gasped. "Och Henry, that sounds dreadful. Was he still alive?"

"Yes, but barely. When I approached him, Roger opened one eye and told me he couldn't move his arm."

Henry shifted and stretched his legs. "I attempted to move him, but his screams stopped me, so I just lay next to him for the rest of the night."

Elizabeth sobbed quietly and held Henry's hand. "Ye truly be a hero, Henry."

Henry kept his eyes focused on the ground and didn't reply. "When the sun came up, I knew Roger would never survive where he was, so, with some effort, I pulled him out of the bush and carried him down to the river."

"Good Lord," I muttered. "That must have been an ordeal."

Henry made a heavy sigh. "By the time I got him to the riverbank, it was late afternoon and too late to return. Roger was unconscious, but still breathing. I couldn't leave him, so I built a fire, and we spent another night together. He was conscious the next morning and we talked about what to do next. I decided to cover him with leaves and brush to conceal him from scavengers while I went back to get you...." Another sigh led to tears and a sob. "But Roger grabbed me with his good arm and reminded me they would eat him alive before I got back."

Henry gave Elizabeth a plaintive look. "That's when I knew there was no other way. He would die a horrible death once I left, no matter how I tried to hide him. A rock to the head. A quick and sure thing." The three of us passed a moment of silence.

Elizabeth began to cry, but she waved him on when Henry hesitated. "Go on," she sobbed.

"I tried to tie his tunic over his eyes, but Roger would have none of it. He told me he wanted to watch. To make sure.

"While I looked for a rock, a shadow swept over us and a condor swooped low across the river, its fearsome red eyes looking straight at us. When I returned, Roger lifted his head and screamed, DINNAE MISS!"

Henry looked heavenward. "I remembered your remark, Elizabeth, about a string of shallow graves leading south. But Roger didn't die on account of an accident. I saw the boulder teetering on the cliff's edge above the trail. Two figures were holding on to it. They had been waiting for the right moment."

"Were they natives?" I asked.

"I assume so," Henry replied. "I couldn't make out any distinguishing features other than they stood upright and worked together to move the boulder." He paused a moment. "They did appear heavier than normal, I'd say. More massive-like. Unlike the wiry natives we saw in Buenos Aires, I can't be sure."

Henry made a point of getting to the river first when we reached the sandbank where he had buried Roger. "Stay back!" he shouted. "The condors have made a mess of things. 'Tis not a pretty sight." He blocked our path and held Elizabeth's arm.

"It dinnae matter. I need tae see what's left o him." Elizabeth struggled against Henry's restraining grip. "Let me go! He was faither's friend." Gone was her impatience with Roger's indiscretions and her disappointments. "I must tend tae him," she insisted.

Henry released her and he and I stood back while Elizabeth approached Roger's remains alone.

The stones covering the shallow pit had been shoved aside and what was left of Roger was scattered around the sand bar. Only the flies found enough to feed on.

Elizabeth called out. "John, Henry, help me bury

him again." We found her gathering up Roger's remains. "Deeper this time."

While we worked, a murder of crows cawed in the tall trees around us.

When we were done, I sniffed the air. "I smell smoke."

The wind had been picking up all day, and when we gathered around Roger's freshly covered grave, dark clouds hid the sun as it sank behind the mountains.

"A campfire, perhaps, upriver somewhere." Henry waded out to his waist to get a view. All around him, raindrops hit the river's smooth surface, each drop making its own circle.

He splashed back to shore, shaking his head. "I can't see anything. I guess we should determine what to do next."

"Most decidedly so." I looked at Elizabeth for a response.

But Elizabeth was silent. Rain dripped down her face and hair in rivulets and she ignored the wet. "Every decision I have made has led tae death," she said. "Please dinnae ask me tae make another."

I sensed by her body language that her confidence was losing traction. *What did it matter*? I asked myself. A positive attitude at this point meant ignoring the facts. I knew her faither's warning about putting the lives of his colleagues in danger was haunting her. I took my eyes off her weary, sad face and watched Henry as he walked along the shoreline. "I will scout out the source of the smoke," he said.

"Right," I replied. "And bring us back some good news."

"A joint of lamb would be preferred," I said to Elizabeth as Henry headed upriver. The rain was getting heavier, and I scanned our surroundings for shelter.

"We'll all be dead soon enough," she muttered. Grasping her knees up against her chest, Elizabeth sat silently and stared at the river. Her ginger hair, now soaked, hung in disarray, as rain continued dripping down her face and neck.

"I have news," Henry said when he found me hiding under a rocky overhang. Elizabeth was curled up nearby, asleep.

"Did ye find a pot o tea, perhaps?"

"Not this minute. But I did find a promise of food not far from here. There is a cluster of ramshackle buildings, hovels actually, across the river. Faint light emanates from a window, and smoke comes from two chimneys."

"Promises, promises," I sighed. "If wishes were

horses, beggars would ride."

We sat under a rocky overhang, hunched over on soggy, rocky soil, but at least the rain wasn't hitting us in the face. "'Tis a woeful shelter, rejected by all but us," I observed. Henry nodded. The dropping temperature was making us both shiver in our soaking wet clothes.

"Beth is suffering a bout o melancholy." I opened a conversation to distract us from the cold. "I believe the philosopher David Hume suffered such a condition in '29. While ye be scavenging, Beth confided in me that she would prefer tae end her life noo rather than wait for things tae get worse." Henry's eyes opened wide in surprise. "I tried tae comfort her, but she wants ye tae deal her a killing blow first thing in the morning, after we dig a proper grave, just as ye did with Roger. She wouldn't have me do it because she was afraid I would muck up the job."

We were both quiet for a moment, waiting to see the other's reaction. Then Henry chuckled, and soon we were both laughing. Something about the pathetic futility of Elizabeth's request released a torrent of pent-up anxiety in both of us.

It was still cloudy the next morning, but the rain had stopped. "I have changed my mind about taking a rock tae the head," Elizabeth said in response to our curious glances when she crawled out from under the ledge. "A woman has the right tae change her mind." Both of us nodded. "Roger was a good man. Odd at times, perhaps, but honest and courageous, and I have decided 'tis foolish tae take another life after his and Jacob's sacrifice. Even if 'tis only my own."

Henry knew better than to say anything.

The river was running faster and higher. Whole trees and rafts of driftwood bobbed along the torrent. Roger's new grave was hidden under an eddy of murky water.

Elizabeth washed her face and mechanically did what she could to face another day. Her menstrual flow ran unchecked; it seemed like there was nothing dry in the entire world. When she joined us, Henry handed her a share of what was left of our rations. She tried to put on a happy face. "I remember ye noticed smoke yesterday. I hope ye can lead us tae shelter and sustenance today."

Chapter Five

Henry cleared a passage through thick undergrowth as we headed upriver. "It should not take us long," he said despite our slow going along a ravaged shoreline filled with fallen limbs and overturned trees. "The trick will be crossing the river. Whoever lives there must have a way."

I concentrated on avoiding being whipped by vines and branches unleashed by Henry's efforts. Elizabeth doggedly tramped along behind me. Despite the hard going, or maybe because of it, I sensed Elizabeth's spirits improving. "Rising tae the challenge, are we?" I said when we stopped to catch our breath.

"It might be so." Her cheeks glowed pink from

exertion and her eyes were alight. Excited about a quest that took her mind off depression, Elizabeth gave me a quick nod of acknowledgment.

When the cluster of hovels were discernible through the vegetation, a wisp of smoke appeared to be coming from one chimney. The wind had changed after the storm passed, sending the smoke upstream. Henry paused at a vantage point, a wee clearing with a view of the river's opposite bank. "What do you think, John?" he asked. "Friend or foe?"

"The structures do nae appear tae be built by any indigenous culture," I replied. "'Tis in a defensible location, up against that cliff and with the river acting as a moat in front o them. They probably keep any secrets about the river tae themselves."

"They appear tae be Spanish," Elizabeth interjected. She stood atop a large boulder, shading her eyes with both hands, staring at the encampment. "There is a marker in a clearing next tae the hut on the right; it has the Spanish coat o arms inscribed on it. I recognize the shape and orange and red colors."

I silently admired Elizabeth's keen powers of observation and insight. "I do not see any recourse but tae wait here until we get their attention," I replied. "They have tae emerge eventually. I wish we could make a fire. Henry, do ye still have that penknife?"

Henry looked at me in surprise. "Why, yes. Yes, I do."

"Well then, I suggest ye get tae work whittling a spear tae catch us some dinner. And make us a sling that can send a rock across the river. Beth, fetch us some dry moss, kindling, and some long fibers. Also, keep a sharp look-out for some flint or quartz. I will take first watch."

Henry and Elizabeth gave me startled looks.

"What ye be waiting for? Embarrassed tae take orders from an old man?" *I wonder if we can make a sling strong enough tae send a rock big enough to get their attention,* I thought as my colleagues scampered off in different directions.

During Elizabeth's watch, Henry scaled a brown river fish of unknown name next to a bed of coals. "Might as well prepare for the long haul," I said. Behind me were the beginnings of a lean-to.

While Henry worked on the fish, Elizabeth suddenly threw down the reeds she was weaving and screamed. "Over here! Ola! Aqui, aqui! Por favor!"

Across the river, a figure stood in a doorway. It hesitated for a moment, looked in our direction, and went inside.

"Bloody Hell!" Elizabeth screamed when the figure disappeared. "He saw me. I know he did."

"We're not at war with Spain, are we?" Henry asked.

"Nae since '08. However, we have nae been very cordial since. Just be thankful they are nae French."

"They know we are here," Elizabeth grumbled. "They canna ignore us forever."

Henry chewed on a boney bit of fish. "Maybe they are hermits. This place is not on any map. They may not have seen Europeans for quite some time."

"All we can do is wait until they decide tae be neighborly." I returned to my lean-to project. "We have nowhere else tae go."

We woke up the following day to find a note attached to the lean-to. Written in Spanish along with some broken English, it took some time to translate. "It is some kind of greeting." Elizabeth pointed at the first word. "This is the word for 'welcome,' I think. They want tae know where we are from, hence the question marks. And if we are sick. I am relatively certain 'enfermo' means 'sick'."

Two figures appeared later that day. They stood in front of the hut and waited; their eyes focused in our direction.

"Nae enfermos." Elizabeth shouted. The two men waved back. "Somos de England." The two men continued to wave. "I do nae know the Spanish word for Scotland, but they probably know England," Elizabeth whispered.

The two men conferred for a few minutes, then one of them pointed upriver. "Síguenos," he shouted and walked in that direction. "Follow!"

"He wants us tae follow him," Elizabeth said. "Should we go?"

Henry raised his eyebrows in mock suspense. "What do you think? They might have us for dinner for all we know."

I smiled. "I suggest we follow along until we feel otherwise."

"¡Vengan por Aqui!" A voice rang out from behind us after a half-hour march up the river. The vegetation had become so dense we lost sight of the fellow.

"He is calling us. Something about 'this way'." Elizabeth said.

When we finally found him, the man stood motionless. "Crucen, por favor," he shouted over the crashing sound of rapids. "Cross here!"

"He wants us tae cross, but where?" We could not see any sign of a passage or portage.

The river was narrower now, with swift running water cutting through rocky channels too wide to cross.

"Look at this." Henry pointed at two slots in the rock that appeared to have been gouged out by some tool.

I stooped to look closer at the slots. They were of similar shape and size, about two feet apart, and were located at the rock's edge beyond which the river rushed through a deep channel. When I stood up, the man was busy using ropes to lower a crude ladder across the channel nearest the far shore.

"Henry, Beth. Our guide is assembling a bridge." As we waited, the man retreated and returned with another ladder—this one he laid across a second channel. Now there was one channel left between our host and us. The process was repeated a third time, and once the ladder's top was secured into the slots, the man jumped from rung to rung as agile as a cat. When he reached our side of the river, he smiled and extended his hand.

"Greetings, madame." He gave Elizabeth a gallant kiss on the hand and bowed. "We have been expecting you." His head covered Elizabeth's forearm with a mass of greasy black hair.

"I do nae recall getting an invitation." Elizabeth pulled back her arm and retreated to the security of us, her colleagues.

The man replied with an insincere smile and a blank stare. He had on a soiled work tunic and torn trousers. A full, unkempt beard covered his face except for his intense blue eyes and a long, tapered nose. He was barefoot and his wiry frame vibrated with intensity. I saw no sign of a weapon, but I wondered if the man was under the influence of some drug.

"I am Manuel Esperanza, commandant of the trading outpost, Puerto San Julián, claimed for His Majesty, King Felipe the Fifth. I speak English a little. Pardon my efforts."

Before anyone could reply, Manuel turned and pointed at the ladders. "Move across. Rápidamente, por favor. I will follow and remove the...the...how do you say it? Escaleras?"

"Ladders," Elizabeth replied. "I dare say, 'tis an interesting construction."

"And effective," I added. "It would take some doing tae cross this torrent without them." I wiped the mist off my glasses with a cloth when we reached the opposite side. Admiring the construction, I wondered who or what they're trying to keep out.

Manuel Esperanza, commandant of the hitherto unknown trading outpost, Puerto San Julián, led us along a faint track that snaked through dense vegetation. Henry kept on the heels of our host. I followed Elizabeth. My ankle complained as I tripped over an assortment of obstacles trying to keep up with the fast pace, but this was not the time to trifle about annoyances.

Off to our left, the river hurtled through the jungle, rushing her way into the arms of her mother, the ocean. How quickly things were changing. Too quickly, in my mind. I hated the powerless feeling of being swept into a maelstrom, especially on the heels of a tousled, barefoot stranger with wild, blue eyes.

From a vantage point high above the cataract, three pairs of eyes followed Manuel and his guests as they crashed through the undergrowth. "See his blood-red hair," the eldest one said. "He travels to the temple, as the prophecy foretold. The others hinder his way."

Manuel stopped without warning when he reached the edge of a clearing, causing Henry to nearly bowl him over. "Silencio," Manuel hissed. He pushed Henry back into the brush and stood with one foot in the unprotected sunlight staring into the clearing.

Elizabeth and I struggled to catch our breaths without making a sound. I crept up behind Manuel and followed his gaze, but all I could make out was a wall of vegetation and gray rock.

"What do ye see?" I whispered.

Manuel shook his head. "See nothing," Manuel murmured. "They smell us."

"Who smells?"

My question was ignored. Manuel kept looking at the rocky crags above us like he was searching for something, and by the anxious look on his face, I guessed it was something menacing. He raised his hand at us to stay put as he took one step into the clearing. He took another step and followed the perimeter.

As I waited, swatting mosquitoes, my ankle took the opportunity to remind me how unhappy it was, having swollen to nearly twice its normal size. "Damn," I muttered. "I hope we're nae being lead on a wild-goose chase."

Henry smiled back at me with a twinkle in his eye. "Wild goose stuffed and braised, perhaps?"

I was too miserable to think of a suitable answer, but Elizabeth was quick to whisper back. "All ye men ever think about are yer testicles and yer stomachs. I hope, for once, something comes of it. The stomach part I mean."

When Manuel reached the far side of the clearing, he motioned for us to follow his footsteps, staying close to the vegetation. Henry and I shared a glance when we both heard a high-pitched whistle.

"There it is again," Henry said, still looking at me over his shoulder. "I'm convinced it's some sort of communication. Like a signal."

I nodded back. "I think Manuel feels the same way. And we're not helping him elude whatever it is."

A stockade of posts and stakes appeared through the tangled vines at the clearing's edge. We all quickened our steps. Two men opened the stockade gate as we approached, but there were no words of welcome. Nonetheless, we three ragged castaways gave a collective sigh of relief as we entered the sanctuary.

Five cabin-like structures took up a corner of the enclosed space. The cabins were made of a combination of milled lumber and unfinished logs. We passed through a heavy door and entered the largest structure, a common room built with an interesting assortment of materials. The floor and walls were constructed of crude planks laid in parallel ranks. But all the windows had glass panes and were enclosed in finished casements. I got the feeling the building was put together from castaways. The Spanish Imperial flag, with its vivid red and orange stripes, hung across one wall. I could see blue sky through chinks in the wood-shingled roof, and there was a collection of longswords, cutlasses, and sabers stacked in one corner.

"I smell stew," Elizabeth said the moment we entered the room. "Chicken stew tae be precise."

The aroma came from an iron pot sitting on a bed of coals in a crudely built fireplace made of sticks, clay, and stones.

Elizabeth gave Henry a nudge, "Nae wild goose, but close enough."

"Stew mixed with smoke," I added. "Nae

respectable mason would take credit for such a hearth,"

Elizabeth ignored my bad manners while Henry ogled the weaponry.

"Dinnae touch," I cautioned Henry when he stepped toward the weapons corner. Manuel kept quiet, but his attention focused on Henry's every move.

Henry hesitated, then glanced at our host.

Despite his naivete, Henry could be perceptive at times. He smiled at Manuel and pointed.

"You have quite a cache of weapons, sir. I recognize some English...."

Manuel dismissed Henry by changing the subject. "We take our meals here," he said while marching us toward a side door. "This way." He pointed and gestured for us to exit through another door.

I would have liked to tarry a bit and smell the chicken stew a while longer, but we were encouraged to enter an adjoining cabin.

"I am sorry, Senora, for these, how do you say, habitations?" An oil lamp swung from a rafter at eye level. The room was obviously used for storage but was cleared to accommodate two hammocks and a fancy rope bed. Sacks filled with unknown provisions and a stack of cordwood were piled against two walls. Roots and what looked like dried meat hung alongside the lamp. The room contained a few amenities: a pitcher, a loaf of dark brown bread on a plate, a candle, and some clean clothes were sitting on a pine table. The rope bed was isolated from the hammocks by a tapestry. The lamp's sputtering light gave off the scent of whale oil.

"Nae apologies necessary, el commandante." Elizabeth fingered the tapestry's heavy fabric. "The tapestry is quite beautiful."

The embroidery was carefully done. Flemish, I thought. The two hammocks each had straw mattresses and stained pillows. They looked like heaven and I longed to lie down.

"Dinner is at sundown. You will hear the bell." Manuel spoke over his shoulder as he turned to leave. "Rest." He pointed outside, "El agua esta afuera."

"Why the stockade?" I said as Manuel reached the door.

He stopped and turned around. "Savages live here."

Henry spoke up. "But why were we never...."

Manuel shook his head. "We talk at dinner. Until then." He made a brief bow and left.

Elizabeth leveled a look at Henry's and my questioning faces as soon as the door closed. She tore off a hunk of bread like a rude Scotsman and didn't bother with courtesies. "Do nae start," she said through a mouthful of bread. "I want tae clean up and have a nap before dinner. I recommend ye do the same." She moved the tapestry to cover the view of her bed. "John," her voice now came from behind the modesty panel, "do me a great service and fetch me a bucket o water."

Manuel had changed for the occasion and wore the tattered remnants of what was once a military uniform. Two men assisted with serving what looked to be a stew of chicken meat and vegetables. They spoke only to Manuel in rapid Spanish.

"We are what is left of a trading outpost." Manuel explained. "It was located at a harbor, Bahia San Julián, a day's walk from here on the coast."

"Why did ye move?" Before he could answer, I raised my glass and toasted him with a compliment. "The stew is delicious, as is the wine. Thank you for yer generosity. Ye made judicious choices about what tae salvage."

Manuel lifted his glass along with the others. "We moved after we were forgotten by Madrid. The shipping lanes changed for some reason. No ship has dropped anchor in Bahia San Julián for many years. Without the ships and trade, the natives grew bold. We needed a ... a fort?" He looked at Elizabeth to confirm he had used the right word. She nodded. "The harbor is no longer safe."

All three of us took in the enormity of Manuel's statement. After our enthusiasm at finding civilized inhabitants, it was now apparent our fortunes were only slightly improved. Home was no closer than it was the day before. I pointed to the flag.

"Ye appear tae remain loyal subjects o the Spanish Crown."

"We remain loyal subjects, as you say, and believe the time will come when God and the Holy Virgin will have mercy on us and return us to our homeland."

"There is little likelihood even God will find ye," I muttered while carving a piece of chicken. I gave Elizabeth a glance that said she didn't have to translate my comment.

Manuel took a sip of wine. "We have left messages at Bahia San Julián, but we no longer travel there. The journey is too dangerous." He looked around the table. "Violent savages who live in the mountains sometimes attack us. They are cannibals." Manuel crossed himself.

"Ye said ye were expecting me?" Elizabeth asked.

"We were informed of your arrival." Manuel resumed eating and offered no further explanation.

The three of us put down our utensils and waited. There was no way that comment was going to go ignored.

After a lengthy moment, Manuel pointed his glass in Elizabeth's direction. "On account of you, madame, and your beguiling red hair. The natives with whom we still trade tell us you are a powerful witch. You are fortunate you were not attacked by the cannibals."

Henry's face turned pale, and he pushed his chicken to one side of his plate. Elizabeth touched her hair. "I assure ye, they have nothing tae fear; I am a scientist. Red-haired, perhaps, but not a witch."

That explained the weapons and the stockade. While helping myself to another chicken leg, I turned my attention toward Elizabeth. "Did Magellan encounter cannibals?"

"Aye," Elizabeth replied. "Pigafetta's journal mentions them as well as the giants. Drake included an eye-witness account o how they harassed his men when he wintered here in 1578. But I assumed after two hundred years, both the cannibals and giants would have all died out by noo, either by some European disease or massacre o some sort. I expected tae find bones, nae flesh and blood."

Manuel cleared his throat and interrupted our private conversation. "The natives tell us you are victims of a shipwreck. Are there any other survivors?"

"There are no others," I replied. "But first, please tell us, have ye had contact with giants?"

"Giants?" Manuel looked to Elizabeth for clarification.

"Gigante," Elizabeth reached up above her head.

"Gente Gigante."

Manuel shook his head. "It is the subject of myths." He paused and looked out a window.

He seemed to be choosing his words carefully. When he resumed, he talked very slowly.

"When we trade with them, the natives sometimes talk about creatures roaming the mountain tops—lost souls from ancient times. They say the creatures wait for a savior who comes from a distant shore to rid them of us Europeans. I have never seen such a thing, myself. Proceed with your story, por favor."

Elizabeth's explanation about our expedition and the search for evidence of giants generated dismissal on Manuel's part. "Maybe Magellan saw something, or thought he did," Manuel concluded. "Sailors like to tell imaginary stories."

Manuel's denial of the giants' existence cast a pall over the rest of our dinner. When everyone was finished, Manuel stood up. "Enough for now. We will have more discussions tomorrow. I wish you a good night." He pointed at one of his two companions. "Pepe will lead you to your room."

"What happened?" Henry said after Manuel's quiet helper left and shut the door behind him. "You think we offended him?"

Elizabeth, palms up, shook her head. "He's keeping something from us." Her voice trailed off as she walked behind the tapestry.

"I wonder who the biggest threat is?" I removed what was left of my worn-out shoes and lay back on my hammock. "The Spaniards, the cannibals, or the giants."

Elizabeth peeked around the tapestry. The lamp picked up the amber color in her hair. "Manuel may be mysterious, but he's a gracious host. Dinnae forget where we were last night, and the many nights before that." She closed the tapestry. "For the moment, I have a full belly and a dry place tae sleep. I'll let ye both worry about tomorrow."

The eldest one took his position of leadership outside a circle of giants. He stood inside a deep cave hidden in the mountains behind Manuel's outpost. The others stood in silence, all of them swaying slowly from side to side. He spoke inwardly to the others and made no sound. "We are bound by the prophecy told to us by our fathers and passed down from fathers before them." He advanced toward the circle. The others stopped swaying and kneeled, heads down. The wind howled as he removed a lanyard from around his neck and placed it over the head of one of two young ones who kneeled closest to him. The young one touched a brass key attached to the lanyard. "The great warrior has returned to the temple just as our ancestors foretold. It is upon you to read the tablets and fulfill the prophecy. Prepare yourself."

The one who had been selected stood and backed away. He turned and was gone.

The elder one then sat among the others and curled in on himself.

"I smell eggs and bacon," Henry murmured.

I turned in my hammock and saw shafts of sunlight streaming into the room through gaps in the log wall. The temperature was already climbing beyond comfortable.

"Everybody up-a-daisy," he said.

Elizabeth and I gave back less cheerful replies.

At the common room's dining table, breakfast was a mixture of Spanish biscuits and cakes, strange-looking plates of greens, and what looked like fried pork along with fried eggs. Manuel came and went while we eagerly sampled all that was offered. I was impressed by their culinary skills given their isolated circumstances and it was hard to conceal our enthusiasm.

"Tell us about the trail," I said the next time Manuel appeared. "We followed a well-traveled trail covered with both shod and bare footprints."

"A trading route," Manuel replied. "In the past, we traveled to the villages to barter. Now it is too dangerous."

Henry picked at the hunks of meat and put a piece up to his nose. "I hope we're not sampling a local denizen," he whispered.

"Do not worry," Manuel interjected. "Your breakfast includes native foods. We have chickens and pigs." He picked out a stringy bit of meat with his fingers. "This is chinchilla; tasty, don't you agree? Pepe cooks it with chilis and Pingo-pingo." He winked at Elizabeth. "Pingo-pingo is called the potion for love. El Amor. You understand?"

Elizabeth avoided Manuel's leery stare and concentrated on her breakfast. "My compliments tae the chef," she replied and raised a fork of chinchilla. "Very succulent. Now, ye be telling us about the trail?"

Manuel dropped his stare and frowned. "As long as we have goods to trade, the nearby natives are friendly." He paused for a moment and looked out a window. "But we have limited resources, you see, and the natives depend on us to protect them from the cannibals' attacks. We must be careful how we manage our stores."

A stream of rapid Spanish came from outside. Its pitch made the message sound urgent.

"You can excuse me." Manuel got up from his chair

and stepped out of the room.

"What's going on?" Henry asked Elizabeth. Once Manuel was gone, Henry left his chair and examined a saber from the corner of the room where the weapons were stacked. 'Sheffield' was engraved across the hilt.

"Something about animals. I think I heard the word 'escapar' which means 'escape'."

I took off my spectacles and cleaned the lenses. "I wonder if we should take our leave." I waited for Elizabeth's reaction. "That is, if we can trust that yer beguiling ginger hair will gain us safe passage."

"From here?" Elizabeth chewed and swallowed another mouthful of chinchilla and what looked to be grilled potatoes and onions. "Already, John? What ye be thinking?"

"I think there is a catastrophe waiting tae happen. Manuel's refusal tae address the subject o giants seriously indicates he is either delusional or, as ye say, Beth, he's hiding something. Either condition is dangerous for us. After what happened tae Roger, I believe we are putting an uneasy peace tae the test. We are a burden tae him unless he uses us in some way for his benefit."

"Piece by bloody piece, eh?" Henry made a couple of practice swings. The long, tapered blade whistled in response.

Elizabeth shook her head. "Leave tae where, John?"

I wondered what price Manuel could bargain for Elizabeth's scalp. "'Tis clear tae me Manuel will never allow us tae leave, and we don't stand a chance overpowering him and his men. But if we could escape unnoticed, perhaps by orchestrating a diversion, a fire, for example, and we took sufficient supplies for sustenance and for barter...." Beth's skeptical look interrupted my thoughts. "I know 'tis a chancy plan, but I believe we either get back on the trail or face certain death."

"But the natives! At least we can negotiate with Manuel. The natives will hunt us down like dogs."

Henry swung the saber again; its blade scraped the ceiling. "I wonder where he keeps his muskets and powder?"

"Brilliant idea," I replied while keeping a careful eye on the swinging blade. "Let's split up for the day. Find out what we can."

Chapter Six

"I offered to help reinforce the stockade," Henry said that evening when we shared our day's observations. "But Manuel would have nothing to do with me."

"Bad news." I wondered what the incident was doing to Manuel's state of mind. He had ignored us all day while he and his men feverishly repaired their stockade. From the little Spanish I could fathom there had been an incursion. The pig pen had been damaged and many of Manuel's pigs were butchered, their remains scattered about the stockade's interior. Whoever did it was not looking for food. It looked like a gesture of defiance.

Later, we huddled around the lamp in our converted storage shed, munching on table scraps. In the excitement of the break-in, some of breakfast had not been cleared off and Elizabeth purloined pieces of chicken, bread and vegetables that were left on the table. Sadly, the wine was nowhere to be found.

"I looked for medical supplies, but found none," Elizabeth lamented. "Did ye find the muskets?"

"In a fashion," Henry replied, followed by a pregnant pause.

Knowing Henry's flair for the dramatic, Elizabeth and I indulged him with a moment of suspense.

Henry continued after slowly chewing through some chicken gristle. "With Manuel and his men busy working on the stockade, I reconnoitered unobserved. They store their powder in a big chest. 'Tis covered with copper sheeting, for God's sake. Bronze hinges. 'Tis not proper storage for gunpowder. It looks more like a cargo container, specially made. The thing must be six feet square and looks impregnable. I found it in a shed on the far side of the clearing, all by itself."

"How do ye ken it holds gun powder?" I asked.

"For one thing, the shed is as far from the rest of the compound as possible, indicating combustible storage. I also found black powder smudges around the box's hasp and lock. I did not find any firearms, though."

"The box is unguarded," Henry went on. "Manuel must figure it is too strong to be tampered with. Interestingly, there are slow matches hung about the shed walls and a long fuse has been fitted through one side of the box. The other end is coiled next to the door. It's as if the box was prepared to be ignited."

"I wonder if the fuse is a defense mechanism," I mused. "Of last resort, perhaps."

Henry gulped. "Last resort is right. I estimate that if the box is full of powder, the explosion would flatten the whole compound and much of the surroundings."

"Dread the thought," I replied.

"And another thing," Henry added. "The lock looks odd."

"What do ye mean?"

"Well, 'tis beat-up and made of iron. It doesn't fit in with how the rest of the box looks."

"It was unloaded on the beach while we were still at Bahia San Julián," Manuel said when Henry and I inquired about the box the next morning. "Men dropped it on the shore and left. No word." Manuel described the ship as having triangular, lateen-type sails, two masts, fore and aft rigged.

That seemed strange. I had little knowledge of maritime subjects, but I remember hearing that lateen, or Latin-rigged ships, were used mostly in the

Mediterranean Sea, around the North coast of Africa. Manned primarily by Egyptians and Phoenicians, I think. Manuel didn't know where the ship had come from.

When Henry asked about the strange-looking lock, Manuel cleared his throat and frowned. "A key was tied to a brass lock," he explained. "Later, the key disappeared. So, we replace the lock with one we salvaged from a wreck. I keep the key."

Henry nodded and gave me a sidelong, acknowledging glance.

I sampled a politeness portion of the porridge we were served. "Was there anything inside the chest?"

"Clay tablets covered with pagan symbols. We left them on the beach." Manuel looked out a window that viewed the stockade. "The devil's work."

Henry smiled politely and leaned in my direction. "Probably ancient relics. Imagine the price they would fetch," he whispered.

The next day started with a squeal of delight when Elizabeth discovered the common room had been decorated with Christmas garlands and a crèche. A wee pine tree, decorated with paper cut-outs filled the room with a fresh pine scent.

"Happy Christmas!" we all said, taking in the festive holiday surprise. I had completely forgotten about

Christmas, not only because of the chaos in our lives, but also because of the warm weather.

"Today is the day before Christmas," Manuel replied, accompanied by a smile. "Christmas Eve. Correct? Tomorrow maybe we are dead, so we celebrate when we can."

That evening, our holiday feast consisted of a roast chicken with a gray, lumpy substance that reminded me of the porridge we had earlier. The lumps seem to be a tuber of some sort. Not exactly a potato, but a close approximation. Cups of an amber liquid added a bit of alcohol-infused cheer, followed by a headache. Nothing tasted as it should, but nobody complained.

After dinner, Manuel and his men joined us in Spanish and Scottish carols. Try as we might, though, the jolly songs were only a bitter reminder of hearth and home. We toasted, hoping for better days to come, but after sharing Christmas felicitations, we retired for the night less assured about our future than ever.

The incursion had put me on guard, but I was lulled into complacency with the advent of quiet days that turned into weeks following our Christmas celebration. An early autumn, coupled with Manuel's gracious hospitality, made a strong argument to continue delaying our escape. My ankle took a turn for the better while I lulled about and gained weight.

Elizabeth got Manuel's permission to explore the grounds inside the stockade for evidence of giants. "He won't allow it unless ye be accompanying me, Henry." Elizabeth told us while we lay in our beds after a quiet evening meal. A gleam in her eye gave away her excitement. "'Tis nae a large area, but we might uncover evidence o their presence during an earlier time." She frowned. "'Tis a nuisance, but I had tae agree tae keep my hair hidden under a hat."

"Fine with me," Henry replied. He gnawed at the corner of a hardtack biscuit. It was perhaps the last remnant we had of home. "Maybe we'll find another footprint."

Elizabeth rolled her eyes. "Behind yer jesting, I hope ye see the importance o this opportunity, Henry, my dear." She gazed out our window with a dreamy look on her face. "After everything seemed so hopelessly lost, noo we get a second chance tae engage in an expedition o discovery. A wee one, perhaps, but an expedition nonetheless."

I wondered if Manuel had an ulterior motive for giving Elizabeth permission, but I put my paranoia aside. "For now, I see nae other option than tae placate our host by making ourselves as useful as possible," I interjected, "until a time and opportunity comes that offers us a chance to escape."

"And you're just the man to do it," Henry replied, slapping me on the shoulder with a grin. "Mollify them with your good cooking, witty conversation, and wise counsel while Elizabeth and I scour the compound for giant footprints, or whatever." He winked at Elizabeth.

Elizabeth rolled her eyes. "There's no stopping him," she sighed.

While autumn turned into winter, Elizabeth and Henry did their best to conduct a crude survey under deteriorating conditions and I passed the time experimenting with native ingredients Manuel had stored to concoct European-style equivalent dishes. I often conferred with Pepe, using sign language and a few simple words, to learn more about his culinary success with native plants and animals. I came to learn Pepe was a quiet, introspective man of few words and a reluctant cook. I enjoyed his muted company and over time we established a fond friendship built around cooking and gardening.

When weather permitted, I also enjoyed working the soil. Unlike Scotland's peats and forest soils, the jungle soil was a shallow combination of clay and decaying organic matter. I thought the continuous rains must have washed out most of the nutrients. To compensate, I focused on wee plots and after removing the native vegetation, I turned over what was left, supplemented with organic waste, and topped it off with any additional soil I could find.

It was a slow, laborious process, but I found the hoeing and digging not an unpleasant pastime. The sensation of pressing soil through my fingers elicited emotions I didn't know I had. To further ameliorate the damage caused by erosion, I constructed miniature drystane dykes to check runoff. The activity reminded me of the many hours I spent as a child helping my faither repair drystanes bordering his pastures outside Edinburgh. Revisiting childhood memories was an unexpected pleasure that helped pass the time.

I quietly gave thanks for our good fortune, as confining as it was. For if we hadn't stumbled upon Manuel's outpost, I was certain we would have long since died of starvation, exposure, or God knows what.

"What happened here?" I asked Manuel while we tramped along a path. It was a bracing, blowing afternoon, and I followed Manuel as he inspected the settlement's perimeter. With time on my hands, I redoubled my efforts to uncover a possible escape route. Maybe it was boredom, but I felt a change in the air, besides the change in seasons. The Spaniards appeared tense. Their heretofore cordial manners were replaced with unfriendly frowns and baleful stares. In front of us, five stone monuments were lined up alongside the perimeter wall. Each one had writing chiseled into the face which, I assumed, identified the remains, but the work was so crudely done it was impossible to discern the names. Behind the graves, three logs in the perimeter's wall were tilted out of alignment. *I need tae investigate these logs.* I thought. *See if they can be moved enough tae squeeze through.*

Manuel stopped in front of the wee cemetery for a moment. "Savages attack. With poison. Curare. Do you know of this poison?"

"Asphyxiant." I held my hands to my throat to mimic the poison's effect.

"Si. From a plant."

"Horrible."

"Five good men." Manuel crossed himself.

"Do ye feel like yer being watched?" Elizabeth asked during one afternoon's long siesta hour. We were sitting alone in the common room next to the fireplace. Outside, a breeze brought with it the smell of weather. I tried to appear attentive while fighting off a nap.

"I canna shake the feeling somebody is watching me," Elizabeth went on. "Anytime I go outside, I'll see a branch, or something shift out of the corner of my eye."

I sat up and tried to shake the cobwebs out of my

mind. "I suppose."

"What does that mean?"

"I have nae noticed such a sensation, but 'tis probably because these sex-starved Spaniards get more entertainment observing ye than me. However, since ye mention it, I suppose Manuel *is* keeping a close eye on all of us."

"I found a pistol." Henry said later in our sleeping quarters. I had fallen asleep while studying a Spanish language bible I had found in the common room's library. Henry's announcement woke me with a start to find him holding the pistol like a prize.

"Is it loaded?" I asked.

"Aye, it is. And it comes with some flints and ball." Henry held the pistol in the weak light; its metal pieces shined. When he pulled back the cock, I was surprised how loud it was.

"Where'd ye find it?"

"In the common room, under some rags. I think someone was cleaning it and forgot to put it back in storage. It only has enough powder for two shots, though."

"Don't!" I hissed, as Henry placed his finger in the trigger guard.

"French. Good mechanism," he said, admiring the

weapon.

The discharge shook the room and filled it with smoke.

"Oops!" Henry looked at me wide-eyed in surprise. "The trigger is more sensitive than I thought."

"What the bloody hell was that!!?" Elizabeth screamed behind the tapestry.

"Load the pistol and grab yer things," I said. "There's nae time tae lose."

Once the preparations were completed and the chosen one was ready in body, mind, and spirit, he repeated the first three stanzas of the prophecy as he moved from shadow to shadow, following the scent, and keeping the wind in his face.

Gilgamesh granted us the totality of knowledge of all.
He saw the Secret, discovered the Temple,
he brought information from before the Flood.
He went on a distant journey, pushing himself to exhaustion,
but then was brought to peace.

Go to the Temple where Gilgamesh has returned,
the mighty warrior whose hair is the color of blood.
Approach its walls and examine its foundation, inspect it thoroughly.

Find the copper tablet box,
open its lock of bronze,
Take and read out from the lapis lazuli tablet
how Gilgamesh went through every hardship.

At the natives' camp, the cooking fires were lit. He would wait.

When it was dark, he stepped into their fire circle. An instant later, the natives lay at his feet, prostrate, like the petals on a daisy. "Come with me, my children," he said. "Come with me to the Temple."

The chosen one stopped when the pistol noise disturbed the jungle night. Behind him, a hundred natives froze in their tracks. He'd heard similar sounds before, and he'd watched natives fall and die in the aftermath of those sounds. Recognition turned to thought, then to resolution, and the chosen one accepted the fire stick's consequences of pain and death. Gilgamesh spoke to him. *You will read the tablet about my every hardship.* He held up his hand and the natives crept slowly into the jungle, carrying their bows, arrows, spears, and vials of poison with them.

"What's the hurry?" Henry primed the pistol, and we crept out the door into the chilly twilight of the crescent moon. The open space was in front of us, a black hole partially illuminated by thin moonlight and a starry sky.

I pointed in the direction of the stockade wall and gestured to Henry to keep his voice down. "Firing the pistol made enough noise tae wake the dead." I was tempted to punctuate my remark with an impatient oath. "I wager ye have roused Manuel's suspicion about our intentions, and he is probably looking for us at this very moment." Under the cover of a passing cloud, we dashed across the open ground. "We either make a break for it noo or endure Manuel's wrath." When we reached the stockade wall, I sidestepped around Elizabeth, putting her in between Henry and me. I handed her a leather thong. "Tie up yer hair and cover yer head," I whispered.

"Ye be annoying me, John," Elizabeth hissed back. "Nobody can see my hair color in this black night."

"Dinnae be so sure," I replied. "These people are more accustomed to darkness than we are."

We stopped when we heard cries and shouts coming from the river.

"A war party," Henry murmured. "They sound like renegade sepoys."

"A party for whom?" I replied.

"For the Spaniards, of course."

An arrow whistled out from the shadows behind us and slammed into the wall just above our heads.

We dropped to the ground. "Be ye certain of that?"

I said and got back to a crouch. "This way. Quickly. Stay close tae the wall, in the shadows. There are some loose logs behind the headstones."

"Stop! I command you!" Manuel charged out of the guest quarters, yelling into the darkness. He ran across the open space toward the wall, exposing himself.

Henry crouched and aimed at the running figure, but an arrow got to Manuel first. Nobody moved as he dropped to his knees, struggling with words he knew we could hear. "She must be sacrificed, or we all die."

A native sprang into the open area, grabbed Manuel's hair, and before the dying man could say another word, the native decapitated him with several brutal strokes using a large knife. The warrior clutched Manuel's dripping head by his hair, screamed, and ran toward the gate holding his gruesome trophy high in triumph.

"The poor man," Elizabeth whispered as we continued along the stockade wall.

"It is yer scalp they are after," I replied. "Keep yer head covered. There must be more coming."

"I thought they were afraid of me."

I stopped for a moment. "They may be afraid of ye, but yer scalp is another thing altogether. I assisted in yer faither's studies about the role of totems in aboriginal societies. Once the scalp is separated from the witch, it becomes a totem, an emblem, ye might say, very powerful."

We saw another movement and watched a figure approach the storage shed. He staggered into the structure, carrying a smoking slow match. Arrows followed him in.

"I suspect that is Pepe on a one-way errand," I whispered. "Hurry." To myself, I regretted the loss of my only friend outside of our group.

The chosen one had leaped across the rapids with one native under his arm. While he put the native to work handling Manuel's ladders, he touched the key that hung from his neck. Then, as the natives crossed the cataracts and fanned out into the compound, he walked through the guesthouse and smelled Gilgamesh's blood. The scent led him to the perimeter. He stopped at the smoky storage shed and eyed the box. "The tablets are here." He wondered about Gilgamesh's whereabouts. "I must carry out the prophecy. Gilgamesh will join me when I open the tablet box."

We forced a gap in the wall behind the headstones and wiggled out. My ankle resumed its complaints and I hobbled behind Elizabeth as we stumbled our way down river. "My guess is that Pepe had enough time to light that fuse with the slow match."

"God help us if that powder box blows," Henry muttered.

Elizabeth clutched at her scarf as we scrambled over boulders and loose rock. I had no idea where we were headed or what waited for us. As morning sunlight streamed over the river, I only knew we had to distance ourselves from the explosion that was sure to come. Maybe if we reached the shoreline there might be something –.

A massive bipedal figure appeared ahead of us. "Stop!" I shouted. "We have company." The sound of Henry's pistol being cocked distracted my attention. When I looked again, another bipedal figure, not as large, but half again Henry's height and weight, appeared from behind a boulder to our right. Both figures approached us without making a sound. Their facial features were partially hidden behind hair, but what I could see was remarkably human, on a monstrous scale. Both figures stood upright and walked with very human-like movements.

I was mesmerized by their presence. They were so unreal in appearance, so outside the norm of conventional presumption that I was unable to do anything besides stare.

"Don't shoot!" Elizabeth grabbed Henry's arm and

knocked the pistol out of his hand as both figures approached us. "They're giants!"

The pistol clattered down among some boulders and discharged harmlessly.

"Damn," Henry scolded. "You just sealed our fate."

Elizabeth ignored Henry's oath and froze in her tracks. The dawn's early light caught her face. Mouth open, she gazed at the older giant with a look of delight and wonderment. "After all we've been through. Here they are as if oot o thin air."

"Beth, remove yer scarf and shake out yer hair," I said. "Stand tall. It may be our only chance."

I got down on my knees. "Henry. Get out of the way. Let them see Elizabeth."

Standing alone, Elizabeth shook her head and her fiery mane of hair blossomed out from under her scarf. The larger figure immediately dropped to one knee.

"We are in the presence of Gilgamesh," he large one said in a voice that only his kind could hear. He repeated two lines from the prophesy:

He went on a distant journey, pushing himself to exhaustion

but then was brought to peace.

"Proceed." He pointed at the smaller one. "He has

no more need for guardians."

The deafening sound came first, and we instinctively dove for cover. Channeled by the river gorge, the blast followed, rocketing downstream and knocking down everyone and everything that had been standing. Behind the shock wave, a deluge of debris, rocks, and body parts fell from the sky.

A blue-black cloud carried by the wind filled the gorge and climbed skyward.

I woke up buried under rubble. Worried about my condition and the condition of my friends, I slowly lifted my head to assess what damage I could from my limited vantage point. Nothing moved. Then like a fanciful vision, the larger giant shrugged off a blanket of rubble and slowly got to his feet. He stood motionless, then toppled backward, like a felled tree, his hands holding the sides of his head. To my right, the wee giant lay prone under his own cover of rubble and did not move.

A constant, painful ringing in my head dulled my senses. Coughing from the smoke, my spectacles were gone and my eyes watered. A rain of shredded vegetation and splintered wood fluttered around me. "Henry, Beth," I whimpered. They didn't respond.

Don't do anything rash. I moved my arms, pushing aside loose rocks and rubble. My limbs responded with difficulty. A tingling sensation ran down my left side as I tried to push myself up—a bad sign.

Lifting my head clear of the rubble, I looked blindly ahead of me to where I last saw my friends and repeated "Henry, Beth," a little louder. My view consisted of nothing but unfocused and unrecognizable gray objects of different sizes.

We'll die here, I said to myself. *We dinnae even have tae worry about a shallow grave.*

A shadow crossed over me. Then another. "Bloody hell," I moaned. "Vultures."

Three miles off the coast of Bahia San Julian, on an unusually calm day in early April 1751, the captain and crew of the brig Sophie watched a dark cloud rising from somewhere inland. The Sophie was in search of a scientific expedition that had left Scotland a year earlier. The expedition's ship, the Cumberland, was supposed to return to Scotland after delivering them to an opportune location along the eastern coast of Patagonia, but it had never returned. After waiting more than six months, in a rage and in fear for his daughter's life, Lord Monboddo commissioned a voyage to find Elizabeth, starting at the only known settlement in the vicinity, Puerto Santa Cruz.

"What is your opinion, Mister Lewis?" Captain Lawrence spoke to his first mate while they stared at the cloud through their glasses. The helmsman, Mister Cunningham, maintained a steady course, south-southwest. Lawrence and Lewis studied the mouth of a river that emptied through a channel between high dunes. A broad beach extended south of the dunes.

"It does not appear to be dust, sir. I see black smoke. An explosion of some sort?" Mister Lewis went quiet and concentrated on his glass. "There are ruins, sir. Just south of the river's mouth. Up from the shoreline. Pilings. Looks like the remains of a structure or structures."

The captain ordered the mizzen topsail braced. Orders flew across the ship's deck as sailors hurried aloft. "Bring her about, Mister Cunningham; I would like a closer look. Mister Lewis, get the longboat ready." The captain handed his glass to the first mate and descended the quarterdeck steps accompanied by Second Officer Grandson. "Do we know who inhabits these parts, Grandson?"

"There are no European settlements in this area to our knowledge, sir."

"Interesting. Yet the pilings and black smoke would indicate habitation, wouldn't you say?"

"Unless they are all dead, sir."

"True, indeed. I propose we take a brief reconnaissance. In case of survivors."

Captain Lawrence encountered a passenger at the

bottom of the stairway, a heavy set, older gentleman dressed only in stockings and a waistcoat covered by a dressing gown. A nightcap sat upon his bald, wigless head. The man blocked the captain's way and refused to step aside.

"What is the meaning o this course change?" The passenger demanded, his face red with consternation. "This is nae time for excursions! Bring the ship back tae its plotted course immediately! We've nae time tae waste!"

Captain Lawrence smiled to hide his annoyance with the passenger's impertinence. He gestured to his Second Officer to leave and continue carrying out his orders. "Good morning, Lord Monboddo," Lawrence replied. "We've encountered an unusual occurrence that just happened on the coast. An explosion, but in an area with no known inhabitants. I've ordered a reconnaissance."

Lord Monboddo ignored the captain and shouted at the helmsman, "Turn this damned ship around! Proceed south on our charted course. On my orders!"

Lawrence bristled and raised his hand, countermanding Monboddo's order. "There will be no change in course, sir," Lawrence replied with a stern look. "I am in command while we are at sea, and you have no authority over my command." He reached around Monboddo and opened the companionway door. "I ask that you return to your quarters." After a moment of uncertainty from both parties, Lawrence glanced at three seamen standing nearby. "Immediately, sir. Or I will have to resort to other measures to carry out my order."

Monboddo retreated a step back. "Ye have nae heard the last o this, Lawrence. My daughter's life hangs in the balance whilst ye go gallivanting, chasing clouds and butterflies." He turned and stepped through the companionway door. "I'll have ye tried and convicted; ye hear me!" He shouted over his shoulder. "Or, better yet, hanged if my daughter is harmed."

"You men guard his door," Lawrence told the seamen. "And don't let him see the light of day until I return."

"Aye, sir," one of the men replied. "He's a hothead, that one."

"The longboat is ready to launch on your order," came a shout from the Second Officer.

Lawrence raised his voice in reply. "You have the ship, Mister Grandson. Keep his lordship to his quarters until I return." He ducked into his cabin, grabbed his pistol and saber, and sprinted to the rail. "Hold your position," he said to the helmsman while crossing the deck. "Lower away!" he shouted.

Lawrence climbed over the rail and dropped into the longboat's hold when it hit the water.

"Pull away," he said. Six men, sitting in their thwarts, stretched forward, dropped their oars, and pulled away.

Lawrence reflected on Monboddo's oaths and recriminations as they approached the river's mouth. *I won't be intimidated by the old bastard's bad disposition*, he thought. *Nevertheless, I'll keep this diversion short. A visual inspection will do—no shore excursions. There's no point in making any more out of this investigation than necessary.*

The oarsmen struggled to make slow headway against the river's current. Standing at the bow and armed with a pole, a crewman fended rafts of debris away from the longboat's bow wave. "Blimey," the young lad of sixteen exclaimed. "The whole bloody forest is floatin' downstream." He gasped when a headless naked torso bobbed alongside the longboat, bouncing against the churning oars. "What is this hellish place?"

Chapter Seven

The morning sun's glare blotted out what little vision I had left, and I stretched my free hand into empty space, searching for something to hold. *I need tae move tae keep the vultures at bay.* I touched upon a wee rock and tossed it. Then another.

Forest sounds came back under the ringing in my ears. Bird cries, a monkey's screech, nothing human, but it was life returning. I wanted to release myself to death, but the thought of being filleted by condors and, worse, hearing my friends joining me screaming in agony wouldn't allow me to indulge in a selfish end.

I tossed rocks as often as I could find them until my reach had cleared the area of projectiles. Something more needed to be done. The sun was no longer in my face, and I squinted into the unfocussed morning light. Another shadow passed overhead. The vulture made a croaking noise as it spied its breakfast. He wouldn't make too many more passes.

Ignoring the likelihood of causing permanent damage, I shifted my body from lying on my back to my right side, facing the river. Not everything moved as it should, and a sharp pain in my leg made me cry helplessly. The effort caused a rockslide, and once my crying was over, I resumed tossing the rocks that had landed within my reach.

"John!" A weak voice punctuated with coughing interrupted my efforts.

"Elizabeth? Is that ye?"

"If yer done screaming, can ye help me? I canna move."

"Where ye be, lass?" My blurred vision picked up movement, enough for me to recognize a hand twitching, the fingers alternately clutching and opening from beneath a mound of loose rocks and dust.

"I'm stuck, John. Help me, please." Bands of red trickled between the fingers.

The shadow passed over me again, this time a little higher. To hell with the leg. What was the point in lying still? I put weight on my functional arm and crept forward by jamming my elbow into the gravel beneath me. A wall of pain grew in intensity as I dragged my crumpled self into the sunlight. There was no time to lose.

Halfway out of the rubble, I stopped and propped myself up on a bloody elbow. To my surprise, the pain in my leg lessened. A wee blessing, but I celebrated the relief with a sigh. "Elizabeth," I pleaded. "Stay still. Dinnae struggle. I'll help ye as soon as I can." *Who am I kidding? Certainly nae Elizabeth.*

Where's Henry? "Henry!" I croaked as loud as I could. Only the parrots and monkeys answered my cry.

Elizabeth's red hair appeared through the dust that covered her head. "Damn it, John!" she cried, starting a fit of coughing. "I'm suffocating!"

After too many excruciating fits of crawling exertion I reached Elizabeth. She lay under a mound of rocks and dirt, but thank God, there were no boulders large enough to kill her. I attributed our good fortune, if ye can call it that, by having distanced ourselves far enough from the blast to be out of range of large boulder-sized movement. "Can ye move at all?" I asked.

"I be trying," she replied after a dry, hacking spit. More rocks tumbled from atop Elizabeth and her form took shape.

I scraped the rocks and dirt off her as best I could

until she sat up, looking like a dusty ogre rising from the bowels of the earth. After shaking her head and knocking dust off her face her eyes appeared. Elizabeth looked over the area. "Where's Henry?" she said.

"Henry? I was just wondering that myself. Where *is* Henry?" He had been in front of me when the blast occurred. His pistol had discharged with no effect. He'd said something, an oath. "I have nae idea," I replied. From what I could see, there wasn't any evidence of his whereabouts. There were no mounds of rock covering a body or bloody trails leading away from our area. "Nae news is good news, I suppose. I hope he's off getting us breakfast."

Elizabeth smiled, and the sight, however blurred, of her jolly, unharmed face made me laugh out of sheer emotional relief, even at poor Henry's expense. Caked gray dust covered every inch of her countenance, making her look like the work of a demented face painter.

"Pardon me for saying so, my dear, but ye look like an escapee from a diabolic pantomime troupe."

Elizabeth spat. "You're nae bonnie lad yerself." Chuckling bubbled up from both of us that erupted into laughter and ended in tears while we staggered to our feet and held each other in a long embrace.

"We need tae search for him," Elizabeth said. "He

could be hurt."

Surveying my unfocussed world for clues, I noticed something else had disappeared. "Henry's nae the only one missing."

Elizabeth looked in the direction I pointed. "Aye," she whispered. "They be gone. Both o them."

"I wonder if it's a coincidence or if there's a connection," I mused. "I don't know how long I was stunned by the explosion, but I wager there was enough time for a rescue party tae come and go withoot us noticing." I looked at Elizabeth's reddish-gray hair. "But why take Henry?"

Midday found us by the riverbank. The journey to the river was torturous for me, but Elizabeth was in better shape than I, and she half-carried me down the embankment to the water's edge. With no apologies, we removed our clothing and, like in the Book of Genesis, washed, and cleansed each other with the innocence of Adam and Eve. We used our undergarments as washcloths and took turns rinsing off the thick layers of dust and dirt. Try as I might, even under as adverse circumstances as this, I couldn't stop myself from blushing as Elizabeth's caresses and her uncovered beauty aroused my loins. Man's sex drive is truly unquenchable.

Elizabeth only giggled at my pathetic old man's

manifestation of lust. "I'm surprised ye can find pleasure in my discouraging condition," she said, eyeing the color in my cheeks and the rigor of my penis.

Her playful repost to my embarrassment made me blush even more. No matter how old, a man's fragile ego is often the first casualty from his lechery, thereby closing the door to the enlightenment of romance.

We separated to answer nature's calls in private. While I waited for my sedentary bowels to move, an unusual sound interrupted my sordid thoughts—the unmistakable rhythmic sound of splashing on water, like pulling on oars. I was experiencing a fantasy of epic proportions. After succumbing to a tempest of lust, I had lost my mind.

What's next? I thought. *The Scots March on parade? Do I hear bagpipes*?

"Do ye hear that?" Elizabeth gasped; her nude figure framed by bull rushes. We were indeed children of nature now. Naked and unafraid, addressing each other like wild animals.

I sighed defeat from my efforts to relieve myself and stood, annoyed at the intrusion. I was sure I heard bagpipes. "Did ye hear the Scots March?"

Wide-eyed, Elizabeth gesticulated in the direction of the river shamelessly revealing the pearl-white mound of her left breast. "Are ye daft? There's a longboat!

Heading upstream! Get out here, and hail them!"

I was confused. An agitated naked woman had pierced my bagpipe fantasy bubble. I hobbled from my toilet to the river's edge only to see a blurry rank of pipers marching atop the river's surface disappear from view. I took a deep breath. "Ahoy!" I croaked, mostly for Elizabeth's benefit.

Elizabeth approached me from behind, semi-clothed, still agitated. "Bloody Hell!" she cried. "I will run upstream and intercept them. They canna have gone far."

I shook my head. "No need to exert yerself." I made no effort to conceal my undressed self. In truth, I enjoyed the newfound freedom of being one of nature's subjects. "What goes up must come down. They will return."

Elizabeth's eyebrows furrowed. "True." She gave me a concerned look. "But are ye nae the least bit surprised? 'Tis a longboat, John. An English boat. From where did it come? Are they looking for us? Are we to be saved?"

I was having a difficult time differentiating one fantasy from another. Aye, I remember the sound of splashing on the water. And I admit oars made more sense than a Scottish regiment marching across the river's surface. But how could either scenario be possible? Are we getting rescued by a floating phantom?

Elizabeth took a step back. "Whilst we wait, might I offer a suggestion?"

I nodded and wondered what she had on her mind.

"Would ye mind donning yer clothes? I'd like to make a good impression for our rescuers."

Alas, I thought. *Our bond with nature had come to an end.*

Elizabeth kept her eyes glued upriver and paced back and forth along our tiny strip of sandy beach while I dressed. "Ye better be right, John. If we miss them, we'll never—"

"There's no other way for them tae go," I snapped. "Why dinnae ye spend some o yer frustrated energy looking for Henry?"

Elizabeth stopped. "I would, but, frankly, I dinnae trust ye."

I smiled. "Ye dinnae think they would stop for a broken-down old man? At least I have clothes on."

"Nae silly. But one person could get distracted and miss their passing. They will be moving quickly, downstream. Three eyes are better than one." Elizabeth smiled. "Begging yer pardon, of course."

I smiled back and squinted. "Aye, lassie. My vision is indeed compromised, but I willna let ye down. By the bye, it would be a blessing if ye can forage us something tae eat during yer search."

The shrill sound of my name caught me dozing on the river's bank, thinking about Edinburgh while bathing my ankle in the river. The river was still filled with debris. Elizabeth had scoured the shoreline but could not reach the compound. "The destruction is extensive, and the stench of death is everywhere. I could nae make oot a search party." She gave me a sour look. "Have ye seen the launch?"

A tremendous crashing noise took our attention before I could reply, and two figures approached through the foliage surrounding us. "Henry!" Elizabeth cried. A screech of surprise immediately followed her shout of welcome, for behind Henry stood a giant, half again Henry's height and weight. The creature stood motionless, staring at us with his immense, human-like face, his eyes full of fear and curiosity.

Paying no attention to the giant, Henry jumped across the distance that separated us. "Don't be afraid," he said. "My mate is a peaceful companion."

Elizabeth stood mute, hand over her mouth. "Och, my goodness," she whispered.

For one of the first times in my life I was speechless. Longboats, nudity, bagpipes, and now a friendly giant. My feeble grip on reality was slipping fast.

Henry grabbed my shoulder as I swayed in delirium, my ankle angry at being taken from its bath.

"No need to panic, John. Ben is just as bewildered as you are."

"Ben?"

"That's what I call him. His family name is difficult to pronounce."

Elizabeth suppressed an instinctual feeling of panic by taking a deep breath. She marshalled her courage and stepped toward the giant, hand outstretched. "Pleased tae make your acquaintance."

The giant stepped back, raising his hands in a defensive gesture, palms out.

"Och, dear," Elizabeth said as she dropped her arm. "I feel a sense o apprehension. Strange, though, 'tis nae coming from me."

"Ben doesn't play by our rules of social engagement," Henry interjected. "He is here to observe ... and...." He smiled sheepishly. "Let me explain."

Elizabeth and I ignored Henry, waiting for his companion to do we didn't know what. "'Tis interesting you perceive Ben's feelings, Elizabeth," Henry said. "I can comprehend some of his strong feelings. How about you, John? Do you feel an out-of-body sensation?"

I shook my head. "Nae, thank goodness. I have had too many sensations as it 'tis."

"Ben is here because of a mistake," Henry went on casually, which felt utterly incongruous to the situation.

"Elizabeth and I are similar in size and weight; our bodies, lying on the ground, covered in dust, were hard to tell apart. The giants took me because they were looking for a man they call a warrior with red hair. Apparently, in all the dust and confusion after the explosion, I appeared to be their candidate. I was male, and they didn't take the time to confirm my hair color." Henry glanced at the giant. "After I was transported to their lair, Ben here helped me understand what was going on, if you can call it that. Ben and I could comprehend each other's thoughts just enough to understand one another. The other older giants didn't make any sense at all."

"Looking for a warrior with red hair, aye." I wondered if the warrior was based on a vision, prophecy, or an actual person. A lost European explorer? A Viking, perhaps?

"Imagine my surprise when I regained consciousness to find myself lying on a flat rock looking at a circle of giant apes, all of them jabbering away and pointing at each other like they were arguing."

"They killed Roger," Elizabeth interjected. "Trying tae capture me ... by mistake."

The giant hung his head and swayed from side to side.

Henry nodded. "Something like that. Aye. But the

giants are not killers. 'Twas an unusual circumstance. A culmination of traditions and legends I don't understand."

"A messiah story," I offered.

When Elizabeth ran her fingers through her hair, the giant lifted his head. "What are we supposed tae do?" Elizabeth asked. "Do they expect something from us?" She closed her eyes. "I feel something again. Something that is nae me. But 'tis *in* me." Eyes opened, she spoke to the giant. "How can I help ye?"

The giant looked skyward, and Henry did the same, both of them concentrating on something. "Something bad is approaching," Henry said in a queer, monotone fashion. He turned his unfocussed eyes back to Elizabeth and myself with a grave, far-off look. "A dire crossroads will be encountered soon."

"Might ye be referring tae the longboat?" I asked.

Elizabeth spoke softly. "I believe the giant is afraid." A tear welled up in Elizabeth's eye and tracked down her cheek, leaving a faint trail. "He's afraid the men in the longboat, and those that follow, will kill all o his kind."

The telltale sound of oars splashing on the water interrupted Elizabeth and the three of us looked upriver.

"What's that?" Henry whispered.

"A longboat," I replied.

"A what!?"

I glanced at Henry's wide-eyed look of surprise and shook my head. "I hardly believe it myself. It appeared as if by magic..."

"Quiet!" Elizabeth commanded; her eyes fixed on the giant. "We must let it pass."

I felt a hand on my shoulder and Elizabeth herded me and Henry away from the riverbank into the neighboring brush.

The giant grunted and followed us, his arms wide, keeping us from turning back.

"But wait! Why in God's name...?" I protested, but the giant's bulk forced me and Henry away from the river. Henry meekly obliged, too shocked to resist. Behind us, the splashing drew near.

When we reached a clearing, out of sight from the river, Elizabeth stepped in front of us. "We'll be saved, but nae by them," she said, all the while staring at the giant. "In order for the giants tae save us, I must go tae them," she continued. "They need me, and we need them."

I wanted to say something, but unable to resist our curiosity, Henry and I turned to face the river and peered through the brush. We both gaped, dumbfounded, at the spectacle of sailors, splashing their oars, as they passed an agonizingly short distance from where we stood.

"This can't be possible," Henry said after the

longboat was lost behind the foliage.

When we turned around, Elizabeth and the giant were gone.

long-cut trees just behind the foliage.

When we came around, Elizabeth and the giant
were gone.

Chapter Eight

After Elizabeth disappeared with the giants, Henry and I spent the winter of 1751 huddled inside a dark, one-room shelter erected above the remains of Manuel's outpost. Fortunately for us, the natives who survived the blast – we called them the Ona people – ventured into the freezing wind and sleet and supplied us with victuals and firewood. The blast had felled nearly all the trees surrounding the outpost. As a result, Manuel's clever ladder that bridged the rapids was replaced by enough trees and brush to provide easy access for them to our shelter.

Through the following spring, the keen-eyed Ona children helped us salvage what remained of the stockade, including the iron hardware used in the fireplace. I helped find some damaged but usable pots, but my vision restricted my efforts to find much else of value.

Our most significant discovery was the root cellar, six feet under Manuel's dining room floorboards, filled with provisions and untouched by the explosion. We spent the summer of 1752 replacing our hastily constructed shelter with a more permanent structure over the cellar door.

By the time of the first storm of the following autumn, we had outfitted a passable home with a complement of utensils and tools.

Standing on our stump-for-a-table, Henry scraped and patched the wall with a pewter butter knife, complete with the Spanish coat of arms embossed on the handle. "More daubing, please," he interrupted my thoughts with another of his incessant demands. "And keep that fire going. The daub needs to be thoroughly dry before it drips."

I laid another armful of kindling on our smoldering fire and mixed handfuls of thatch into a bucket of mud. Henry had filled most of the chinks between the wallboards and moved on to the chimney and gaps around our primitive door.

"Dinner tonight will be delayed if I be required tae

prepare more daubing whilst cooking the rabbit stew."

Henry chuckled, his face and hands speckled with mud. "Just add the rabbit and some salt and dandelion weed to the daubing. It'll serve both purposes."

I laughed back. "I wager yer concoction will reduce the threat o breaking wind."

"If only it were true." He jumped to the floor and ran my daub mixture through his fingers. "More mud, less thatch."

Along with his carpenter and builder skills, Henry also turned out to be quite the linguist and had mastered the Ona language well enough for us to avoid misunderstandings. The Ona tribe's survivors, primarily women and children, had been friendly, with one exception, a lone survivor from the band of savage cannibals, Kitchkskum. He was a lean, wiry man with a permanent scowl. I called him Kitch. We felt he pressured the villagers to resist our overtures of friendship. The natives were still too ravaged to follow his influence, but Henry and I knew his hostility would permeate through the tribe before long.

Our rabbit stew was taking its time coming to a boil and ashes fell in the pot every time an errant gust of wind found its way down the chimney. The new batch of faggots did nothing but smoke. Frustrated, I abandoned my post and reached for the brandy. We celebrated when we discovered the full, dusty bottle of brandy in the root cellar, and we've been careful about its consumption ever since. I hoped it would last us through the winter. It seemed a shame drinking such a wonderful libation from an ugly earthen cup, but all of Manuel's drinking goblets were shattered in the explosion. "Do ye still think Elizabeth will return?" I asked after a parsimonious sip. "I be losing hope."

Henry poured himself a comparable amount, sat on the stump, and leaned against the wall. "I still have the same dream. The one where she walks into a clearing that is surrounded with dense foliage, by herself, and clad in animal skins. Looking as much animal as human."

Henry's dream didn't give me much confidence. Elizabeth said the giants would save us. At least that's how I remembered that chaotic moment over a year ago when the giant and Elizabeth disappeared to a place unknown. A moment etched in my memory and my sorrow.

Brandy rolled down my throat, bringing warmth and satisfaction along the way. "I dinna have any dreams, but I keep thinking aboot our last minutes together. Elizabeth and I, waiting for the miraculous longboat from nowhere tae rescue us. Then, before my watery eyes, Elizabeth was gone, the longboat had passed us by, and we be left on our own." I stared at a painting, a landscape, that miraculously survived the explosion, frame and all. I considered it a talisman and hung it on the west wall, over our bed. "It was as if the three of us agreed it was the best thing we could do."

"That's exactly right."

"I beg yer pardon, 'twasn't my idea, I kin tell ye that."

"We didn't have a choice."

I pondered what choice had to do with Elizabeth's departure until Henry interrupted me. "If we had hailed the longboat, we would have opened the gates to European domination, and the giants would all die. That is certain. Since we let the longboat pass, the giants will save us. How and when, I have no idea, but again, I am certain they will."

"I canna remember having that thought. Come tae think of it, I wasna thinking much at all."

"It crossed your mind. That's why you didn't interrupt Elizabeth's abduction. You knew for an instant 'twas the only plausible choice."

I was weary of the conversation. What matters is we sacrificed rescue. It's hard to find comfort comparing our abandoned life to sailing for home.

That night as we lay together, I chuckled in Henry's warm company. "Maybe I also kent that a rescue would have kept us from learning about our love."

I thrilled as Henry's fingers explored my nipples. "See?" he whispered. "We all benefited."

Henry says the Ona repudiate our life of sodomy, so we keep outward expressions of our affection to ourselves. We may be loathsome in the eyes of our neighbors, but I couldn't believe the change in me when Henry and I abandoned pretense and accepted each other as a loving couple. It's not that I love men. Mary is my wife, and I will love, honor, and cherish her for my entire life. The point is I love Henry, and he loves me. Our love has made me stronger, and I am no longer afraid. 'Tis a feeling I would never have discovered in Scotland. I'm surprised to hear myself think such thoughts, but I am a different person now. No one cares about me except Henry, and he loves me for what I am, not for what I was.

I experimented with fermenting after the brandy was gone. My berry-based alcohol concoctions had given us some amusement. The Ona's fermented maize they call chicha was not to our liking, and their mushrooms even less so.

At the edge of the clearing, where I remembered Manuel had a cemetery, we erected a shrine on behalf of him and his men. It was a simple cairn with a wooden plaque at the base and a humble cross at the top. Henry inscribed the plaque with as many names as we could remember. It won't last long, but I felt the shrine's existence would ennoble Manuel's legacy as our benefactor. We had our differences, but I had grown to respect Manuel's civility and hospitality.

That winter into spring of 1752, Henry labored on household improvements, and I spent my time on a second garden project in the general area where I planted my first garden before the blast. I hoped this one would be more bountiful. One afternoon, while I was in the process of erecting a trellis for pea vines, Henry squatted next to me and gestured for the children to leave. "We have company," he whispered—the children scattered in hushed silence.

A tingle went up my spine. *Elizabeth*, I thought.

"Better get on your feet," Henry interrupted my vision.

I slowly stood, eyes closed, savoring the moment, sensing Elizabeth's presence.

"Greetings," Henry said in the Ona tongue.

Why speak to Elizabeth in Ona? I thought when a very un-Elizabethan-sounding voice replied in Ona. Kitchkskum appeared when I opened my eyes. He barked something I judged to be significant by the pitch of his voice.

"He wishes to invite us to a feast," Henry translated. "Tonight. No excuses. At sundown."

I nodded but didn't listen, confused that Elizabeth appeared as an Ona chieftain.

Kitchkskum eyed my trellis with a skeptical look. "He suggests, with respect, that you consider planting something else."

I ignored the twinkle in Henry's eye and smiled in disappointment. "Tell him I shall consider his advice."

That evening Henry rummaged through our trinket box, looking for a gift. We'd never been invited to an Ona gathering before. "What is this all aboot?" I asked.

"He probably wants to ask us something," Henry replied. "Or tell us."

"And he uses a feast tae hide any bad feelings and avoid a confrontation?"

"Very diplomatic, don't you think?"

"All well and good so long as we dinnae become the main course."

"Let us be on our best behavior."

Our arrival was met by an unceremonious grunt from Kitchkskum who pointed at an open space among a crowd of warriors. We sat in a semi-circle facing a bonfire. Behind us were two more semi-circles filled with younger men, women, and children; my blurry view could only make out individuals near me, but I guessed there were about one hundred tribespeople. Henry immediately got to talking with the warriors near him while I smiled and quickly exhausted my Ona vocabulary with my neighbor. Fortunately, the conversations soon ceased when the drumming started. Jugs of chicha passed freely from hand to hand as the drumming increased in volume and tempo. I quickly discovered it was not their usual chicha and after a second helping, I was having trouble thinking clearly. "What are we drinking?" I asked Henry.

Henry shrugged his shoulders, his eyelids drooping. "It tastes like chicha, but there's something else...." A neighbor handed him the drinking gourd. Henry took a modest sip and passed it to me. "Something for special occasions, I presume." He shook his head. "'Tis strong. Go easy. We need to keep our wits."

A line of singing and shouting dancers jumped into the space between us and the fire, clothed in feathered headpieces, capes, and little else. Gyrating feverishly to the beat of the drums, the dancers leaped in a circle that came dangerously close to the fire. Some feathered headpieces smoldered then burst into flames looking like roman candles. Everyone cheered when the headpieces burned, illuminating the area with darting flashes of light and shadow. I grabbed Henry's hand. "Somebody is going tae get hurt." Henry didn't respond but kept a tight grip on my hand. I figured with all the commotion nobody would notice our intimacy.

The chicha brought on visions of colors and shapes, augmenting the wild action around the fire. For an instant, the dancers froze in an eerie silence and members of the audience handed each one a long stick or rod. Then the drumming resumed, and the dancers leaped back to life, twirling the rods above their heads. One of the dancers, his hair under a flaming headpiece, made a wild, animal-like scream and dove straight into the fire, emerging on the far side, smoke drifting off his torso. The next dancer chased after him until all the dancers followed their lead through the fire.

I turned away. "Och, my God," I whined, anticipating the worst.

Henry shook my hand. "Keep looking," he said. "Don't embarrass us."

Mesmerized by the bizarre spectacle and stupefied by the chicha, I gave in to primitive impulses and yelled as loud as the warrior next to me.

The dancers went in and out of the flames until one fell headlong into the coals. But instead of rescuing the poor fellow, the dancers gathered around him, to the sound of more cheering and faster drumming, and pinned him with their rods until the fire consumed him from head to toe.

The dancer's body convulsed for a few agonizing moments before it went limp. Using their rods, the dancers turned him over, exposing charred flesh and bones. The head was burned beyond recognition.

Kitchkskum appeared from shadows beyond the fire pit carrying a long knife. He spoke, the words sounding like an invocation, and while he spoke, he thrust the knife downward and opened the dancer's chest. With the skill of a practiced chef, he removed the heart and handed the smoking meat to a warrior who in turn cut a portion and handed the rest to another warrior. The doling out continued until all the warriors, including Henry and myself, received and ate the proffered sacrifice.

The chicha had by this time immobilized me and I hung on to Henry with all my strength. The taste of the dancer's heart seared my mouth and throat.

"Don't leave me," Henry said.

I assume he meant don't faint since I had no intention to leave him. Gruff, unfriendly hands grabbed my shoulder. I was going to be thrown into the fire—the next course. Speechless with fright, I let out a hoarse cry of distress to my partner, no words, only desperate squeals that fell on deaf ears. My only attempt at resistance was to collapse in the stranger's arms as he dragged me off. I tried to say something before Henry disappeared, but nothing came as my world descended into black.

"Henry?" Instead of a bed of coals, I felt the familiar discomforts of our bed beneath me. Eyes still closed, I reached for my partner, but I was alone in the company of a pounding head, dry mouth, and upset stomach.

"Bloody hangover, huh?" Henry's voice broke through my agony from the far side of our room. He sounded weak. "Have some water, not that it helps much."

I opened one eye and accepted Henry's offering with a nod, which hurt. "Is this what 'tis like to be burned and eaten?"

"Probably worse, I wager." Henry stepped back, not too gracefully. "I'd say we're unlucky to be alive. Hopefully, things will improve."

I love Henry's dry sense of humor. Even under the worst of circumstances I could count on him to see how ludicrous it all was. "What happened?" I finally said after three draughts of water. Sitting up set off dizzy spells, and when the twirling stopped, I fought off the urge to close my eyes. Henry regarded me with a pensive expression. "Never mind." I waved him off. "Pray continue."

Henry took my hand. "That devil Kitchkskum has a

perverse sense of spectacle."

I smiled back, enjoying Henry's touch. "I cudna agree more. But tae what end?"

"To impress us, apparently."

"Scare the bloody hell oot o us more likely. I was far from impressed."

"He wants our help."

I gagged, then laughed in disbelief at the same time. My sternum ached from the exertion. "Help? How in God's name can we help him?"

"His witchdoctor alerted him the giants are returning."

"Returning?" Henry's vision of Elizabeth appearing in animal skins came to mind. "My word, that 'tis news. But 'tis it good news?"

Henry smiled. "I'm not so sure. Kitchkskum thinks we killed those two giants we saw before the explosion. Now he wants our help killing the rest of them. He also respectfully asks that we don't blow up the whole valley this time."

We looked at each other and laughed at how ridiculous that sounded.

"But why does Kitchkskum want tae kill the giants?"

"Prestige. According to Ona legend, the giants had always been the powerful, dominant force in Ona culture until the arrival of the Europeans. The giants disappeared after the Europeans came; remember what Manuel said? Well, maybe Manuel believed what he was saying. Anyway, after Magellan's visit, the natives thought the Europeans became the powerful force in their culture. Until now."

"Until now?"

"Yes. In Kitchkskum's mind, you and I have become the new power."

"Good Lord. The man's delusional."

"Maybe so. But if the giants do return, Kitchkskum thinks they want to retake their power by force, and he wants to take credit for eradicating them and become the Ona chief. My guess is he wants us to employ our explosive magic to kill the giants. Then he'll eat us to absorb our magic."

When we finished laughing, the enormity of Kitchkskum's ultimatum sunk in; we were on Kitchkskum's menu no matter what we did or couldn't do. I flashed Henry my look of concern. "Noo what?"

Henry squeezed my hand. "Stay on Kitchkskum's good side for as long as we can. Hopefully, the giants will help us escape somehow."

"And if they dinna?"

"We'll run for it."

"Right. As I recall, running dinna work so well the

last time we tried."

While we waited for who knew what, I harvested a handful of edible bean pods after three weeks of cultivation plus a vigilant defense against marauding pests, both winged and earth-bound. Most importantly, the efforts kept my mind off our impending doom. Thoughts of Elizabeth were tormenting. If she were indeed to return, I selfishly wondered how I was to handle my conflict of affections among her, my wife, and my forever lover Henry?

As the spring season of 1752 progressed into the summer of 1753, I recognized jungle sounds coming from beyond our clearing. I gave the sounds Scottish names as I worked the garden from early morning until the mid-day heat or a storm sent me scurrying back into our home. There was the yellow-billed Dotterel's staccato trumpet, the screeching sound of the Capercaillie, and the occasional low moan of a great-crested Newt, which was only heard in the morning.

I'd thought I'd heard everything when a new sound caused the hairs on the back of my neck to stand. It was as much a sensation as a sound, and I was tempted to get on my feet and search for the source. Instead, I remained on my hands and knees and listened, half inside my head and half out.

I'm not ashamed to admit I've heard voices in my head. It's commonplace for old reprobates like me, often attributed to and laughed about as a sign of feeble-mindedness. But this sound was unusual enough I overcame my embarrassment, and, to my surprise, Henry didn't tease me when I explained what I'd heard. Instead, his keen interest put me off. "What am I supposed tae say?" I complained when he asked me to explain what I'd heard. "'Tis like asking me tae explain the sound o a breeze. When I tried tae grasp the meaning, all I could fathom was the possibility o words."

Henry stared at the ceiling. "They are listening."

"Who has been listening and tae whom?"

"The giants. They've been listening to you out there in the garden. They are telling us something." He looked out our Dutch door. "But why don't they approach me? Why approach us through you?"

That got my hackles up. "Och. Now see here. I'm just as important."

Henry waved me off. "No." He hesitated. "Maybe they think you are a better contact."

"Indeed," I countered. "Remember Elizabeth 'tis among those giants, and she likes me better than ye," I chuckled. "Maybe the only way she can contact us is by transporting her thoughts in the giant's fashion."

Henry chuckled back. "And she is apparently

157

having a hard time getting the hang of it." He picked up one of my snap peas from the table. "They must be aware of Kitchkskum's evil plan." He crunched down and the crisp pea pod snapped in his teeth. "If the sounds come again, listen closely." After a swallow, he nodded. "Tasty, John. What's for supper?"

I was bestowed with the chef's duties through delicate underhanded diplomacy whereby I naively found myself cooking to the tune of Henry's lavish compliments and encouragement. He reciprocated by providing me with scullery implements and sundry contrivances. Our home benefitted from his skill as a carpenter, scavenger, and general builder. Over the dry summer season, he kept busy from morning 'till night, adding an extra room, watertight roof, stone cooking hearth, cistern, chairs and tables, cupboards, chests, and a respectable privy that channeled river water to wash away our waste.

Our stout bed was a focal point not only because it took up most of our living area, but it also represented our commitment to each other. Every time I looked at it, or barked my knee on it at night, I was reminded of our first winter and our coming together as lovers. I'm still unconvinced I've changed my sexual preference; rather it seems I've acquired a greater appreciation of the borders of one's sexual identity. When Henry and I are together, I respond to his presence and his touch as though I've been transformed into something other than Mary's husband. What a scoundrel I am.

I was thinking about Elizabeth three days later when the noises returned, stopping my progress in the garden. Sounds that resembled words. Remembering the conversation Henry and I had about Elizabeth using the giants' method of communication, I considered the noises to be coming from her. *Elizabeth, be ye there*?

The noises stopped.

JOHN!

I recognized Elizabeth's voice the minute I heard my name. It came loud and clear, but from where I couldn't fathom. "Aye, Elizabeth, 'tis me. Where ye be coming from?" I stood and surveyed the area, hoping to catch sight of her dressed in animal skins calling to me in the ordinary everyday manner people use to communicate, but I was alone in my garden.

JOHN, she repeated.

The detached voice sent shivers up my spine. I kept looking and seeing no one.

HENRY AND YE MUST LEAVE.

Mystified by the voice and the message, I made my way to our home where Henry was involved with a woodworking project. "Leave?" I asked.

"Leave?" Henry asked when I walked through the

door.

Eyes wide, I pointed to my head and mouthed Elizabeth.

Henry nodded and sat still, watching me closely.

AN EMISSARY WILL GUIDE YE. FOLLOW THE EMISSARY.

I shook my head. "Emissary? What emissary? Tae where?"

There was no answer. Exhausted from the incident, I stared at Henry. "'Twas Elizabeth. But from where I cudna tell."

Henry didn't seem surprised about the strange conversation. "What did she say?"

I repeated Elizabeth's message, hoping Henry would make sense of it. "Ken ye what her message is aboot?"

Henry stood, walked to the doorway, and studied the open space. "I've been worried how long Kitchkskum will wait for the giants to return."

"So, Elizabeth wants us tae leave whilst we have the opportunity?"

"Precisely. I can foresee Kitchkskum holding us hostage, forcing the giants' hand." He removed the pistol from under the bed. "I hope Elizabeth's emissary comes soon."

Later that day, a monkey, of all things, approached

me while I was gathering berries for supper. At first, I couldn't believe my eyes, having grown accustomed to their poor strength. But after my initial surprise at its presence, we exchanged smiles while maintaining a safe distance. Being in close company with any wild animal larger than a mouse is unsettling and I couldn't help but wonder if the beast had some malicious intent. It didn't look sick or desperate. In fact, it looked quite healthy, leaving me unsure if I could ward off an attack or outrun it to our front door. I made sure my hoe was visible. The monkey was about the size and weight of a seven-year-old child with longish wavy brown hair covering its entire body, a prominent nose and chin, and bright, piercing eyes. I couldn't tell its sex.

"Henry!" I shouted, hoping to get my partner's attention.

Alas, I got no response. The monkey remained silent, sitting on its haunches. He alternately stared at me and then turned his head, looking behind him. I took a step back, in the direction of the house, never breaking eye contact with the primate. He – I took the liberty of assigning a gender – must be looking for food. It was the only explanation. I wished I had a banana.

Two steps more, and Henry appeared at the shelter's door. "John? Did you … What's that in the garden?" An arrow whistled past my head and buried itself in the wall of the house. I looked behind me, and there was the monkey, lying face down, arrows protruding out its back. Behind him were natives, many natives. They stood motionless with Kitchkskum at the front in his warrior regalia.

"Hurry," Henry said. "In the house, quickly." He disappeared into the house and when I reached the door, he stepped around me with the pistol and primed and loaded. "You stay here," he said, "and think about Elizabeth." He stepped outside, the pistol pointing skyward. "I have an appointment with Kitchkskum."

"Elizabeth," I repeated, both aloud and internally, but got no answer.

The sharp crack of the pistol's discharge interrupted my efforts, followed by Henry dashing back in and opening the cellar's trap door. Arrows thwacked against the walls and roof. A thin stream of smoke crept across the rafters.

"Get in," Henry commanded, holding the door. "They'll be on us in a moment."

Chapter Nine

I did what I was told and didn't look back, the fear of death beckoned me on. Henry pushed me into the cellar room and slammed the door shut. "The candles and matches are behind you," he said in the pitch black while bolting the door from the inside. "Hurry up so I can reload."

We knew the door wouldn't hold the natives for long unless … Unless they were afraid of the pistol and intended to smoke us out.

I felt my way around until I got my hands on a candle and matches. It sputtered to life after a few strikes, and I held it high, illuminating Henry's efforts. Fuzzy images of crates and bundles of provisions appeared as apparitions stacked against the cellar walls. Henry lit another candle when the pistol was loaded and gingerly set the pistol on a shelf. "Fill a sack with candles. I'll fill another with food, shot, and powder."

A cool breeze filled the room and exited through gaps in the door, drawn by the fire. The candles flickered. "Quickly now," Henry said. "The fire buys us some time until the house burns out and the natives discover the cellar's opening. We need to be gone by then."

Manuel's cellar was a marvelous feat of engineering, considering what he had to work with. The room was easily ten feet square with six feet of headroom, situated directly under the original living space. He took great pains to excavate the cellar a considerable distance below ground level, a precaution that saved its contents after the powder blast and was saving us at that very moment, hewn by hammer and chisel out of solid rock. A passageway, a tunnel really, led from the cellar to points unknown. That was where the breeze was coming from. We had explored the tunnel, but never took the trouble to find an outlet. The breeze proved there was one ... Somewhere.

The tunnel's headroom was considerably less than the cellar, which contributed to our futile attempts to find the tunnel's end. Once provisioned, I crouched through the tunnel's opening, Henry behind me.

"What was the commotion about?" I asked while we crawled by candlelight through the underground passage.

Henry extinguished his candle. "I shot Kitchkskum. In self-defense, mind you. He had his bow at the ready before I could get a word in. My guess is once he killed the monkey, he wanted to intimidate you by killing me."

"The monkey?"

"Elizabeth's emissary. Unfortunately, he arrived too late to help."

We were past the distance of our earlier reconnaissance, into unknown territory, dark as a coal mine and challenging to navigate. The only assurance we had of a destination was the breeze in our faces. Water dripped down the sides of the tunnel and our path took on a slippery incline. It was getting difficult to hold the candle and keep my footing.

"That occurred to me," I replied. "But I was so distracted by the unusual sight, all I could think was avoiding being bitten."

"Instead of thinking about Elizabeth." Henry stopped and whispered for me to stop as well. "Be still. I want to listen."

Scraping sounds gave the pursuing Indians away. They were some distance behind us, but it wouldn't take them long to cover the distance.

"We're better off now that the tunnel is getting narrow," Henry whispered. "They won't be able to use their bows or throw anything from here on."

"That's heartening. Should I extinguish my candle?"

"No. They know where we are. We'll save the darkness for a surprise defensive tactic. A pistol shot in the dark might spook them."

I strained my neck looking up for a light source. Could the tunnel just be an air shaft? But why make it so large at the cellar then taper off to a crawl space at this end?

An arrow bounced off the tunnel's wall and skidded to a stop at our feet. Then another.

Henry asked for the candle. "Here's where we make our standoff. I'll send them a greeting."

After the third arrow, Henry's pistol discharged with a crashing roar, the percussion sending lose rock and dirt tumbling down from the space ahead of us. "Ye have opened something!" I exclaimed. Daylight filtered through the cloud of dust. My heart leaped to think an exit might exist after all, covered by fallen debris.

"Another round, if ye please," I told Henry, leaving my bag of candles behind. "I shall scramble up and dig."

More shafts of light filled our perch and Henry's second discharge gave me time to clear a hole large enough for us to wiggle through. No more arrows came our way.

We emerged into a clearing bordered by walls of solid rock twice our height and covered with dense vegetation. The only sound was birdsong and a breeze passing through trees high above us. Without a word spoken, Henry and I set to work sealing the tunnel's exit with whatever we could find. Our covering would not hold back a concerted effort, but it would buy us time, and our pursuers would be at a distinct disadvantage.

The clearing looked to be untouched by anyone for a long time. Vines and tendrils snaked down the rock faces and the few gaps we could see in the rock were shrouded in green.

Henry paced around the clearing's perimeter, tugging on vines, and investigating the gaps. He stopped only long enough to reload the pistol. "We have to leave soon," he said. "Look for a handhold. Anything."

In the end, I climbed on Henry's shoulders and hoisted myself over the rim of the rock wall with the aid of vines. My limbs ached from the exertion. I lay back and took a deep breath in preparation for the next stage of our escape. Two gasps later, Henry's pistol discharged again with another mighty roar. My heart sank when war whoops followed the discharge.

"Run!" Henry shouted.

I wasn't about to abandon my mate and I peered through a thicket near the rim. Henry had moved to the opposite side of the clearing and had grabbed some vines when arrows hit him multiple times. He fell without a sound into the arms of those savages, and they dispatched him mercilessly with their hatchets and knives. No sooner had they finished with him than they were scrambling up the wall, blood lust in their voices.

I stood frozen in grief, unable to turn away from the horrible sight of my Henry scattered in bloody pieces. Henry had sacrificed his life to save me from capture and certain death, and I couldn't let him down, but where to go? There were no trails, so I stepped into the lowest growth of brambles and ran headlong through an out-of-focus green unknown, my useless eyes full of tears. It was hopeless. The savages would have an easy time of it finding my trail. I had only moments left before I'd follow Henry's fate.

A rocky outcropping blocked my way, and with the savages' screams approaching, I decided then and there to end the chase. *This is nae going to end well*, I thought. I hadn't the strength to defend myself even if I had the means. All I could do was face my pursuers, stand resolute, and accept my fate. I thought about Mary and Henry and how much they meant to me when I was swept up from behind by a powerful force and carried like a ragdoll above the foliage, flying from one outcropping to another. Overwhelmed, I shut my eyes and gave my life up to God's will.

"John? John, wake up." Elizabeth's voice, soft and sweet, wafted into my subconsciousness.

I must be in heaven. Is she wearing animal skins, I wonder? Nae in heaven, I suppose. Probably a beautiful white gown with wings. I hope she kept her red hair. Nae o the pictures I've seen o angels included one with red hair, but why nae? I hope Henry is nearby. He couldn't possibly be in Hell. Dear me, I'm too afraid tae look.

A very unangelic shove to my shoulder disrupted my reverie. "Yer faking it, noo enough o this nonsense. Open yer eyes."

She wouldn't say that in heaven. I reluctantly squinted and Elizabeth's stern visage appeared. Eyebrows down, she moved her head to one side, her red hair swaying to the movement, just as I caught her gaze. "He's awake," she said. There was a rustling, and I sensed movement, but there was no reply.

Elizabeth smiled. "Nice tae see ye. So sorry about the circumstances."

Where was I? I was lying on a comfortable bed. The cushioning was soft, but it didn't feel like animal skins. It was a large, airy room. Sunlight streamed in from above my head. I tried to sit up, but Elizabeth restrained me with a firm hand on my chest. "Nae yet, my friend. Just relax. We have some catching up tae do."

"Henry's dead," I said, causing tears to well up in both eyes. "He saved my life. Sacrificing his own."

Elizabeth nodded and placed a cool hand on my forehead. "I morn his loss as much as ye. We loved him dearly." She slid a blanket up to my neck. "I'm so glad we got ye out in time. We are all that's left." A cloud of red covered my face as Elizabeth leaned over and kissed my cheek. "Ye need to recover yer strength. Noo rest."

We loved him dearly, she said. I shuddered to think about the love Henry and I shared. Ours was a love shunned by society, but just as deep and compassionate as any other. Would I ever share that love with anyone else? I was afraid even Elizabeth would despise me if I told her.

Elizabeth lifted my head and tipped a cup of warm liquid to my lips. "This will help."

Half in and out of consciousness, I dreamed of Edinburgh and Mary and my days as an assistant clerk at university, quietly studying botany, long before Henry set me free to a life of confidence and strength. Could I go back to that? Overcome by a tailspin of despair, the dream dissolved into darkness.

The next morning, Elizabeth's voice broke through

the darkness as though a curtain had been opened. "Good morning, John. Would ye care for a cup o tea?"

Her words were so incongruous under the circumstances I laughed despite my contrary mood. She sounded like a hostess in a manor house on the outskirts of Aberdeen. "Och, that would be splendid," I replied, in my best posh manner.

Elizabeth laughed back, either with me or at me, I'm not sure. "'Tis good tae hear yer laugh again. There's still hope for us."

My laughter died as quickly as it appeared. "Hope for us? Peter left us for dead and we obliged, one after another. Two shallow graves along a dusty trail, just like ye said, Beth. Henry was our last hope, and he dinnae even get a grave. Nae, Elizabeth, there are nae more plans tae make or risks tae take." A wave of remorse rolled over me. "All we have left are memories and haunting dreams."

My whining was answered with a sigh. "I must leave, but only momentarily. Enjoy yer breakfast."

The morning light illuminated a bedside table and a bowl filled with a brown gelatinous mass next to a mug filled with a beverage. The beverage smelled familiar—a berry I had used earlier while on the trail. The bowl, however, had a foul odor. "What in God's name?" I chewed on a spoonful and gagged. It was a cold barley-like mush, filled with long, greenish fibers.

As disgusting as it was, the mush energized me, and I gained the strength to find a door that led outside to a meadow bordered by a ring of hedges. When I stepped off the threshold, I squinted in the sunlight, and once I was accustomed to the glare, the view was remarkably sharp, like I had a new set of eyes. *My God, I can see again!* While I studied the surroundings, Elizabeth appeared, walking toward me, her arms gently swaying at her sides. Behind her, a line of giants stood motionless, like sentinels, their eyes glowing from behind dark facial hair.

Clad in a long, loose gown that flowed around her, Elizabeth's ginger hair sparkled in the morning sun, and an aura of complementary colors encircled her. "Are ye ready tae return tae reality, John?"

Elizabeth's form became soft around the edges. I instinctively rubbed my eyes, fearing I was losing my sight again. "Reality has nae been kind tae either o us, Beth," I said, dropping my hands from my face.

The noises came back into my head, and I thought of Henry and me in our home laughing, holding, and loving each other. I felt the warm thrill of his touch on my arm, bridging the void that exists beyond thought. My knees buckled, but I didn't care.

"John!" Elizabeth's commanding voice interrupted

my reverie. Henry's touch turned cold. "Dinnae leave!"

I wanted to hold on to my lover and never let him go, but Henry faded away. Elizabeth's voice scattered his presence like leaves in a gust of wind.

"Our work is nae yet done," Elizabeth continued. She pointed at the circle of giants. "Our hosts need us."

I felt overwhelmed with grief seeing Henry again, almost touching him. All I wanted was him back, but all I got was nonsensical gibberish. "What hosts? The giants? What do they need us for?"

Elizabeth took a breath, still pointing at the stoic line of giants. "We are guests in their world. A world that exists at the crossroads o dreams and reality. With their permission, we see them both as physical beings and spirits. Spirits that transcend logic and science, time and space. The spiritual essence o giants is deep-seated in our imaginations — a legacy mankind inherited from our ancestors long ago."

Henry remained an ache in my heart, but I quieted my frustration, returned my attention to the leader of our ill-fated expedition standing before me, and made an honest effort to understand her strange story. "Is that why Henry appeared so real tae me?"

"Henry and ye were indeed close in the giants' spiritual world. But ye need tae –"

A giant approached us from the edge of the clearing,

easily eight feet tall, his hair a mixture of brown and gray strands. He looked angry and even though he was mute, his commanding thoughts drowned out Elizabeth's words. *Enough! This one with the red hair is here to fulfill our prophecy. You are here to facilitate what Red Hair is about to do. Nothing more.* No noise, no gibberish, his words rang clear and precise in my head.

Eyes downcast, Elizabeth accepted the interruption and gave a submissive nod. I summoned my courage to look into the giant's eyes. "What prophecy? What do ye want from us?"

The giant looked heavenward, and his thoughts took on a chanting, poetic pace. *The great warrior, Gilgamesh, smeared with the blood of his enemies, will return to his homeland and smite the pestilence that comes from over the edge of the sea.* He gestured at Elizabeth. *Gilgamesh's time has not yet come, but our enemies will not wait. Red Hair will fulfill Gilgamesh's prophecy.*

I tried to hide it, but I couldn't help but laugh. "Have ye been taking lessons in swordplay then?" I asked, smiling at Elizabeth. The ensuing uncomfortable silence was deafening as the giant rocked back and forth on the balls of his feet and Elizabeth kept her head down, refusing to look at me. The giant's anger swept over me like a wave. He was near the edge of violence.

"That 'twas a stupid thing tae say, John. And

uncalled for," Elizabeth said later when we retired to her quarters and stared at bowls of brown mush. The same glop I'd gagged on at breakfast. We took seats at the wee table, and I grunted in disappointment.

"Dinnae they have anything else tae eat?" I whined.

"Dinnae change the subject." Elizabeth raised a spoon full of glop to her lips. "He might have killed ye for yer insolence, and I wouldn't been able tae stop him." She swallowed, and I noticed the slightest grimace cross her face. "Ye have nae idea how powerful these people are."

I froze, spoon in mid-flight. "People?" I replied after a moment's hesitation. "They're people noo?"

"They are every bit as human as we are." Elizabeth returned the spoon to her bowl and wiped her mouth with a brown woven napkin. She picked up a fruit of some kind and, while holding it, looked me in the eye. "We are o the same species."

I decided to try the fruit. It couldn't taste worse. "And how do ye ken that?" I asked, selecting what I hoped was a ripe one.

Elizabeth wiped her chin with the back of her free hand as she bit into the juicy fruit. "I'm pregnant, that's how."

"What in God's name did ye just say?" I pushed back my chair, dropped the fruit, and stared at her, open-mouthed.

"Ye heard me. I'm pregnant with a giant's bairn." She put her hand on her abdomen, a maternal move I'd never seen her do before. "'Tis been two months noo. I dinnae ken when he comes tae term."

"But ... But isn't that an abomination? A sin against nature?" I retrieved the fruit and took a bite to hide my astonishment. It was quite good. Sweet, like a peach.

Elizabeth snorted and shook her head without looking at me. "'Tis nae more an abomination than ye and Henry."

Another shock. This one straight to the ribs. I didn't know whether to be angry, insulted, defiant or ashamed. "I dare say Elizabeth the two circumstances have little in _"

"Nae another lecture, John. Please." Elizabeth broke me off with a snarl. She got up from her chair. "Ye canna ken the circumstances."

"Ye have nae idea o the danger ye be in! 'Tis amazing enough ye were fertilized successfully, but if the fetus is anywhere near the relative proportional size o its faither, it might very well split ye open during birth if nae before." I stood and blocked her exit. "Why would ye do such a thing? Have they drugged ye?" I wondered if she was under a spell of some kind. I'd heard of a new scientific study called mesmerism which was being used to induce dreams. Beth mentioned dreams...

Elizabeth shook her head. "I do this o my own free will." Her eyes fill with tears. "I ken the danger." She leaned against a wall and stared at the ceiling, her hand on her abdomen and a frown on her face. "I be taking that chance because ... because I be their only hope, and I be willing tae die tae keep their hope alive."

I took another bite of the peach-like fruit. "Yer speaking tae me in riddles. What hope?"

Elizabeth ignored me. "And now that yer here, ye can carry oot the prophecy if I die."

The sweet juice caught in my throat, and I sputtered, "I canna have a bairn! Even if the faither *is* the same species!" I meant the comment in jest, but I sat paralyzed at the thought of intimacy with a male giant for a moment. I pictured him with Henry's face and a chill ran up my spine.

We both laughed even though we were far from understanding each other. "Ye be a silly goose." Elizabeth returned to her chair and picked up her spoon. "I apologize. 'Tis my fault for nae explaining. The bairn is going tae Scotland." She took a long, slow spoonful of her mush. "With one or, God willing, both o us."

I kept laughing, now in delirium. "Ye call that an explanation? Elizabeth, what the devil be ye talking about?" I stood and grabbed the back of my chair to

steady myself. "Yesterday I witnessed my best friend...."
We made eye contact for an instant. "All right – *my lover*
– get hacked tae pieces by savages. I'm an emotional
wreck thrust into the company o giants who eat terrible
food and can read my mind. Noo, by way of explanation,
ye tell me we be taking yer giant-bairn home tae
Scotland?" I sat back down in front of my bowl, put both
hands on the table, and took a deep breath. "Sorry, but
can we change the subject noo?"

Elizabeth smiled and wiped her mouth. "Aye. Let's
do." She stroked my hand. "That's a lot for one day. Now
eat yer supper."

I stared at the bowl and closed my tired eyes. "Isn't
there something else tae eat?" I knew I was being
unreasonable, but considering the size of these giants,
this gruel seemed woefully insufficient sustenance. Just
a few spices would do wonders, and what's wrong with
some vegetables? I wasn't going to even suggest meat,
figuring I was dealing with vegetarians.

"'Tis all I've been offered," Elizabeth answered.
"I've gotten used tae it and the bairn seems tae be doing
well. Never have I been healthier."

I had to admit my sight had improved, and my ankle
was no longer a constant torment. Was it because of this
gruel? I reluctantly took another swallow. "I'd like tae
meet the cook."

Elizabeth nodded. "Maybe I can arrange that. It could keep ye occupied until we leave."

I paused before waking the next morning, hoping a dream would take me inside our home with Henry's warmth nestled beside me. I never took those first moments before arising for granted. Rather, I would lie still, feel the morning come with all my senses, and relish the pleasure of being alive and in love. Alas, this time my cold bottom confirmed my disappointment. I had felt Henry's presence yesterday; at least I thought I did. But today, no amount of effort brought him back. It must have been a trick played on me by the giants. Can Elizabeth and I be victims of ... I thought for a minute. I had read a treatise by Sir Thomas Browne, something about wandering in the mind. He had a word for it. I believe he called it a hallucination. Even though Beth claimed she acted on her own free will, how can she be sure? What if...

A knock at the door stole my attention. "Come in," I uttered, pulling the cover-up to my chin.

A wee giant, human-sized, entered carrying a bowl of that disgusting mush. I presumed it was a youth. It silently placed the bowl on a side table and laid a spoon and napkin beside it. "Is that all giants eat?" I asked, pointing at the bowl, and wrinkling my nose. The little giant gave off an odor, but I couldn't place it.

He pointed at the bowl, mimicking my gesture. Then he turned toward me and wrinkled his nose.

I laughed so hard I nearly fell out of bed. "Aye!" I cried. "Ye be hating it too!"

The giant lifted his cheeks and bared his teeth, attempting to duplicate my mirth. It was a forced gesture, feigned perhaps, but I felt we had shared an opinion.

The scullery turned out to be a dark, foul-smelling place run by females, all of whom avoided me like the plague. Elizabeth had made good on her offer. I presume it was because the leaders couldn't care a whit. What harm could I do? We'll see. I brought an empty satchel I intended to fill with edibles I'd identified and had used successfully, I dare to say, in our home. The females eyed me with looks of trepidation and kept their distance.

"Dinnae be afraid. I be John, and I be yer friend!" I pointed at my chest, then pointed at the female closest to me. "What be yer name?"

The giant female cowered and looked from side to side at her companions. A noise filled my head that sounded like Beeyochen. "Beeyochen," I responded. "Pleased tae meet ye." I offered my hand in greeting only to be met by gasps and quick steps in retreat.

Through with formalities, I held up my satchel. "I be off tae forage ingredients," I announced. "I shall return."

I was back by midday. As the females gathered 'round, I emptied the satchel and spread my collection of berries and fruit on another tree-stump-for-a-table. "These will improve flavor," I informed my students. "Try one." I held a berry close to Beeyochen and encouraged her to give it a try. Much to my surprise, she accepted my offer and popped it in her mouth.

My new friend, the wee giant, appeared carrying a stack of empty bowls during the taste test. We repeated the smile exercise done earlier. This time it felt more genuine. He seemed to be a quick study, and from that point on, my lessons in the culinary arts went quite well.

I wish I could say the same about Elizabeth's pregnancy. "The bairn gets bigger and more active by the day," she admitted while we sipped herbal tea in her room. Beth lay in her bed, supported by cushions, and I sat next to her. Sunlight streamed in through a window, but not enough to lighten our spirits. Beth's complexion was sallow, almost yellow, her bonnie red hair was in tangled disarray, and she hardly had the strength to sit up. She was four months pregnant now and her abdomen's distended condition appeared as though she was at full term and then some.

"I fear for yer health," I admitted. "There's so much we dinna know. Giving birth is a mystery in and o itself, but this ... this unnatural condition leaves so much—"

Elizabeth shifted her weight to one side and groaned. "The bairn is healthy; that 'tis what matters. I can handle a little discomfort so long as he lives." With her tired eyes nearly closed, she leaned back against the cushions.

I had so many questions. It was rude of me to annoy her, but I was determined to get answers. "I am still mystified as to why ye chose tae have the bairn. Ye mentioned having acted on yer own free will, but ye be sure? Could it be the giants cast a spell o some sort on ye..." I paused a moment. "And, for that matter, maybe me as well?"

Elizabeth opened her eyes and chuckled. "Casting spells, ye say? 'Tis absurd. Do I look bewitched?" She sat up and gazed at me, a look of incredulity in her eye. "Really, John. Ye canna be serious."

I felt a flush of embarrassment. "Well, maybe nae casting spells, but Sir Robert Browne wrote about how the mind –"

She waved me off with a stroke of a hand. "The giants be nae magicians. Their existence is different from ours, ye might say, but they play by the same rules of nature and science as we do. There is nae hocus pocus."

"Yet ye referred tae the fetus as 'he'. How can ye know an unborn's sex if nae by some magical means? Or 'tis is simply some unexplainable insight?"

"Their destiny depends on being saved by a warrior. The prophecy is clear about that."

I shook my head. "My dear friend and colleague, I will nae belabor the point. I will only say that prophecy is nae science."

"Point taken. I appreciate the contradiction, and the irony." She sat up. "Nevertheless, I be long past controversy. The bairn is arriving soon, and he's a boy. That is the state of things at this time." She smiled. "Ye probably wonder about the faither."

The change in subject disturbed me. Aye, I wondered about the faither, but I would never intrude on such a private matter. Still, I didn't object. "Of course, the question has crossed my mind."

Elizabeth lowered her eyes. "'Twas anatomically impossible for me to mate with an adult, so I was paired with a young male."

I looked away, aghast at her disclosure and trying to hide my reaction. I would think even a scientist would hesitate at revealing such information.

"The coupling went on quickly and successfully," Elizabeth continued. "It only took one try." She hesitated, lost in thought. "I canna say the experience was pleasurable. He was inexperienced. 'Twas more mechanical than pleasurable."

"What is the reason ye be telling me this?"

"Ye should know this information. Purely for scientific record. In case ... in case I canna speak for myself." Elizabeth lay back, a satisfied look on her face as if she'd accomplished a difficult task. After a moment, she turned her attention back toward me. "How are ye getting along?"

Surprised at the sudden turn in the conversation, I stuttered an improbable "I've made some progress with my new friend, Pepe."

"Pepe?" Elizabeth winced in pain, then shrugged off her discomfort with a sigh and stared at me with a questioning look. "Manuel's cook?"

I nodded. "Aye, he reminds me of Pepe a wee bit. He's quiet and not very big. A young one, I think. But he's friendly, and we've established a rapport. I can't pronounce the sound he indicates is his name, so I decided tae call him after my late friend. Pepe saved our lives, ye remember that."

A hint of a smile crossed Elizabeth's face. "Yer such a sentimental old scoundrel. 'Tis glad ye be on a first name basis with a giant."

"We've been working together in the scullery. I think he likes my cooking." After what we had just discussed, my association with a giant took on a greater significance. What were the chances? Was my friendship with Pepe planned?

We laughed, and Elizabeth perked up; her face regained some color. "'Tis important for ye tae have an emissary. The older ones dinnae have the patience tae look or listen beyond the boundaries o their philosophies. We are nae more than messengers, and a means tae an end...." She coughed and gave up a low moan.

Two giant females entered the room and attended to Elizabeth, like bees taking care of their queen. They set up a new tea serving when they were done and left as quietly as they came. Elizabeth looked refreshed.

I offered her a mug and we savored the moment. I wanted no more intimacies, so I changed the subject. "What philosophies do ye refer tae?"

"I canna tell ye much, but I ken the giants live simultaneously in two different places; one place is a mystical realm between dreams and reality. 'Tis their preferred home – their safe place. We be there noo. Their other place, the one we know as a physical existence, they consider dangerous and void. But they must inhabit both places. Up until noo, the giants have satisfied their physical existence by dominating the natives who worshipped them. However, that relationship has been under threat since Magellan's time. Manuel's outpost hastened the dissolution; then, the explosion ended the giants' association with the native inhabitants. A

European invasion will end the giants' physical experience. And if they die physically, that is, by the sword, they vanish forever. Nae only dead, John, but their past will become myth … folklore … unaccountable fantasy." Elizabeth gasped for breath and set her tea on the table.

"Are ye well?" I moved close to Elizabeth's side and held her hand. "Is there something wrong?"

"Just a pain," she replied, breathing deeply. "They come more frequently now." She shook her head and focused on me. "Let me continue."

"There willna be anything left, John. Nae bones, nae evidence whatsoever." A tear glistened on her cheek. "And by 'they', I mean nae just the giants among us here, but the manifestation of giants in cultures the world over." She leaned back. "I will preserve their existence through him." She laid her palm on her belly. "All it takes is the physical world's acceptance o their existence. Hidden, perhaps, but living participants in the physical world."

"What makes ye certain the Europeans willna put yer bairn in a zoo or circus, or worse?"

"Because he will look like us. He will grow up tae be a giant among men. The giants thought I was their savior from the Europeans. Me with my blood-red hair. I was supposed tae lead them in battle to vanquish their foes."

Elizabeth sighed. "Well, I was not the savior they thought I was, but I will be in a different way."

"How do we get yer bairn back tae Europe?"

"The Europeans will return as sure as the seasons change, and when they do, we'll take my bairn tae Scotland. Where he will finish what we set oot tae do."

"The Europeans will come back here? This God-forsaken place?"

"Nae, the giants will transport us tae Puerto Santa Cruz when the time is right." Elizabeth smiled. "Maybe nae in a horse-drawn carriage, John, as ye had hoped, but 'twill be a different journey than the one we traveled."

"What am I supposed tae do in the meantime?"

"Och! For God's sake, John," she said with a roll of her eyes. "Teach them how tae cook!"

Chapter Ten

The next day, when I came to Elizabeth's room to resume our talk, her bed was empty and smeared with blood. A pool of blood covered the floor, and from a distance I heard a bairn's cry. Pepe approached me as I steadied myself against Elizabeth's bed, confused and recoiled in shock.

"*Where is Elizabeth?*" I asked in thought.

Pepe's face broke into shards of remorse. *She is gone*, came a voice in my head as clear as a bell.

He. Pepe pointed to where the cries were coming from. *Yours now.*

How could that be? We were just talking, joking about a horse-drawn carriage. Sure, she was tired, but nowhere near death's door. "*Let me see her!*" I demanded, fighting back a sob. "*Let me see Elizabeth!*"

Pepe's face hadn't changed. *Gone*, he repeated, eyes cast down. *No more here.* He lifted his gaze to my face. *See him.*

I was tempted to confront Pepe, accuse him of being the faither, but I was afraid of the consequences. Alone now, everything I said or did was suspect. Did he love Beth as much as I? Would I provoke him with my grief? The question of Elizabeth's end filled me with dread. What primitive ceremonial rite had they done to her? "*Where be her remains?*" I demanded. "*What have ye done with her?*"

The little giant stepped toward a door. *He is all that is. She is gone forever.*

"*STOP!*" I shouted, aloud and within my head. I was crying, desperate for something of hers. I had to accept they had somehow disposed of Elizabeth's body in secret, but I wasn't ready to let her go that easy. "*What about her clothes? Her things? There must be something.*"

Pepe turned at the door's threshold. *Her things you will have. Come.*

Children could be entertaining at a distance, and for short periods, but from my experience, parenting was a costly and demanding ordeal, much to be avoided. There were too many starving orphans roaming the streets already. Despite my perfectly logical argument, Mary always resented my decision not to have children. It was only after many years of bitterness that we agreed to salvage our marriage by avoiding the subject.

Pepe led me down a corridor and I reluctantly followed. What was I supposed to do? Elizabeth told me the bairn was to be taken back to Europe. Ha! Her aspiration seemed so preposterous I scoffed at the thought. Maybe Elizabeth could have got us back, but me? With a wee bairn? Preposterous didn't come close. I was doomed, plain and simple, and the bairn was doomed along with me. If it had any human features, the giants would never accept him. They will banish us, leave us to be eaten by the savages.

I hated to think what went on during Elizabeth's labor and delivery and made a silent prayer for my dearly departed friend and colleague. The thing had crawled out of her womb and shed her like a husk. I wondered if Elizabeth even saw it before she died. What if I killed it? Would that put an end to all this mumbo-jumbo nonsense? Pepe and the giants would surely dispatch me if I did, and I would welcome the end.

The crying stopped when I was escorted to a room furnished with a wee bed. Quilts and coverlets hid everything except for a shock of bright red hair.

"Hello?" I lifted a coverlet and stared into a pair of

blue eyes that stared back with more intensity than I expected. "Och, aren't ye a sight," I spoke out loud.

It gurgled back. A not-so-little hand, hairless and pink, reached toward me, fingers wiggling. And when I extended a finger toward him, its grip was undeniable. The bairn's face wasn't entirely human. I haven't been in the company of many bairns, but common knowledge assured me newborns, at least Scottish newborns, didn't look like this one. It's not even a day old and it shakes my hand in greeting? Gives me a serious stare? What's next? A philosophical discussion concerning reason and nature?

Pepe's voice entered my head. *He looks like you*, with *the other one's red hair*.

I ignored Pepe's patronizing puffery and touched the few remaining gray wisps that lay across my bald head. "And lucky for him."

A female giant entered the room and lifted the bairn to her breast. "A wet nurse," I sighed. "They be taking care of it. Maybe I am nae responsible."

Pepe disappeared and I returned to my room without an escort. Lying on the bed, my thoughts lapsed back to Elizabeth. It was too soon for me to grasp the enormity of her loss, but it was only a matter of time. I was overdue for full-scale remorse, over the loss of so many. Jacob, Roger, Henry, and now Elizabeth. Why me?

Why should I survive? I, the frail one with no redeeming qualities, should have been the only casualty. Now I felt like an accessory to crimes of bestiality and death. Aye, and let us not forget sodomy.

Three days later, Pepe entered my cooking class, and a hush came over the room. *Name bairn*, he announced while I showed the females how to fold spices into a stew. I hadn't seen the thing since that first day and I had put it out of my mind to save the last shards of my sanity, concentrating on the cooking class and grieving for my friends. I still blamed it for Elizabeth's death. Name it? It didn't deserve a name. At least a name I'd recognize. "*Ye name it,*" I replied.

The giant didn't move. *The prophecy foretells human name.* He lifted his hand and the females hurried out of the scullery, leaving the two of us in a faceoff. The enormity of the confrontation was conveyed in Pepe's eyes. They spoke volumes.

I screwed up my courage. *Be ye the faither?* I thought.

You the father, he replied, his eyes losing focus, shielding something. *No other father.* He looked down, breaking our stare. *Only ... only donor.*

The wet-nurse appeared with it in her arms, naked and clinging to her breast. It was already larger than when I last saw it. Its fingers and toes were more fully developed, and its hair was longer. I tried to relegate it as nothing more than a sub-human curiosity, but when it turned its head, its facial features, now more human than before, made it hard for me to dismiss it out of mind.

It gurgled and smiled, its blue eyes studying me with a calm, appraising look.

I knew what was happening. I've been manipulated before, my sentiments played with like a fine-tuned harp. *Even if it appears human, I hae nae room for the thing.*

Name it and he lives, Pepe told me. *He has no other purpose than the prophecy.*

"*What about me?*" I replied.

You have no other purpose than to shepherd him to his destiny.

The enormity of Pepe's threat deflated my resolve. He was right. Another death would not accomplish anything. No matter what it was, it was Elizabeth's bairn. "*What does the prophecy say about me?*"

You and baby go … He stopped mid-sentence, like he was trying to grasp something, furrowing his brows. Then he sighed and slumped his shoulders, defeated.

Go? Were they going to book us passage on a merchantman for quick transport to Edinburgh? When? Is the wetnurse coming with? I chuckled and touched the bairn's outstretched fingers. "Maybe I should name you Prophecy."

The wetnurse placed the bairn in my arms and as I held him close, his warm body comforted mine. Tears came and I succumbed to parenthood.

Back in my room, the bairn asleep in his crib next to my bed, I wondered if I should name him after one of my departed associates. I decided it would only open a wound. "I shall call him Robert," I said, and decided he would take Elizabeth's family name, Burnett. Robert Burnett. Sounded good enough. Giving him my name would raise eyebrows, I suspected, if it ever came to that. He lacked a middle name, though. Perhaps Horatio or some such. I thought for a moment. Elijah might do. A tad odd, though appropriate, in memory of his mother. Robert Elijah Burnett. "Aye. All right, Robert," I said to the sleeping prophecy. "Welcome tae my world."

It wasn't a proper christening, Pepe was the bemused Godfaither, and I had a shy member of my cooking class sprinkle Robert with water while I recited a prayer.

In the name o the Lord Jesus Christ, I lay my hand upon ye and commend ye tae the gracious care and protection o God through all yer days, and may His richest blessing rest and abide with ye always. In the name o the Faither, the Son, and the holy spirit. Amen.

Robert never flinched, nor did he ever take his eyes off me. He was now a person in my eyes. An orphan, to be specific, carrying the legacy of a vanishing civilization that pinned their hopes on him for nothing less than their very existence. At the end of the service, when Pepe placed Robert in my arms, the conveyance filled me with the sensation of a challenging responsibility.

It didn't take long before my responsibilities caught up with me. I was glad the wet nurse relieved me of Robert's unsavory bodily functions, but that didn't excuse me from attending to other matters regarding his welfare, such as companionship, emotional support, and being a playmate. These matters quickly consumed a great deal of my time.

He grew like a proverbial weed with no discernible giant features aside from his astounding physical growth rate and intellectual maturation. In six months' time, the daily routine I had grown accustomed to, gardening, teaching in the scullery, and investigating flora for new cooking ingredients, was thrown into disarray by Robert's demands for attention and stimulation.

By the end of his first year, I introduced him to the arcane thoughts and practices of European culture, leaving his giants' education in the hands of mysterious mentors who addressed him from a different realm. I hadn't forgotten Pepe's prophetic words, "you and baby go," but I was skeptical about what 'go' meant. I knew for certain Europe was not getting any closer.

I often asked myself if teaching Robert about Europe was a pointless exercise if he never would experience it first-hand. "I might as well teach ye about cultures on the moon," I told him one afternoon after a session about Europe's Age of Enlightenment.

"Cultures on the moon?" Robert's innocent face was full of curiosity while the white crescent hung above us in the late afternoon twilight. Robert's brows furrowed, "Ye described the moon as being uninhabited—"

I shook my head. "Nae, nae, nae. I be speaking figuratively. I was comparing the uninhabited distant moon tae the futility o learning about Europe's cultures with nae hope o witnessing them."

Robert smiled. 'Twas his turn to shake his head. "Figuratively, ye say. Yet both the moon and Europe are real places, are they nae?"

"Aye, o course, they are both real. But for us, isolated as we be, their reality lies more in the realm o imagination and conjecture than in actual fact. I can describe European culture tae ye just as readily as I can conjure up a moon-borne culture with inhabitants who be fond o green cheese. I have nae way tae substantiate either premise."

Robert's jaw dropped. He pointed at the moon, but continued to face me, eyes wide in surprise. "Green cheese? But ... but surely ye dinnae mean—"

I gave in to a chuckle and put my hand on Robert's shoulder. "More figurative nonsense, my ... my son." I took a breath, feeling the enormity of my emotional gamble. "Let us drop the subject for now."

We looked at each other for a quiet moment while Robert pondered my confusing allusions topped with my unexpected gesture of endearment.

He cleared his throat. "Ye be nae my real faither, and I be nae yer real son, but like the cultures o Europe and those on the moon, the premise is unimportant. Ye be real tae me."

For days after that conversation, I wondered how and why it turned out the way it did. In a round-about way, we had reached a threshold in our relationship. Acceptance. We were a bonded pair, faither and son. I felt for the first time since Henry died anything was possible.

As the months of Robert's second year passed, we addressed each other as equals on an intellectual level. Physically I prayed he wouldn't grow more than an acceptable size insofar as European standards. If nothing else, if we ever did get to Europe, he stood the chance of having frequent head injuries in our homes and businesses built for people no taller than five feet ten inches. With his help, we had devised a crude substitute for paper, using the ancient papyrus method, a writing quill, and an ink substitute made from rosin and ground minerals. With these tools I supplemented my lectures, introducing the hands-on academic enterprises of learning the alphabet, then on to reading and writing.

"Faither? 'Tis time we visited Europe." Robert told me one afternoon when I paused for a drink of berry-flavored water during my third lecture on the monarchs of Europe. I'd lost all track of time's progression, but by my best estimate, it was Robert's second birthday, March of 1756. Another fall season was starting even though, in my mind, the month still announced the coming of spring.

I was focusing on the influence of Catherine II on Russian political affairs, and I drank slowly to hide the fact I knew not how to respond to his unexpected assertion. I'd learned from experience never to be surprised at Robert's penchant for spontaneous remarks; they were sometimes out of context, but never incongruous. "Yer teaching about European politics," he went on, "has prepared me to engage with yer philosophers, generals, politicians, and scientists."

I took a breath. "The fact o the matter is I dinnae ken how."

Robert cocked his head and squinted, mimicking my weak eyesight, an inside joke of ours. "What is it ye dinnae ken? Ye have explained that the journey begins in a village called Puerto Santa Cruz. From there we board a vessel that sails across a vast waterway tae Europe. I have heard aboot this journey many times."

"True," I replied. "The journey tae Europe is simple in concept. The devil is in the details."

Robert stood and raised both hands in puzzlement. "What is this devil?" He scanned the mountains behind us.

"The devil hinders our progress, son. 'Tis a devilishly long distance tae Puerto Santa Cruz. Ye be going over uninhabited terrain, always in danger of falling and sustaining injury. And the only food and drinks we would have would be what we can carry." Memories of the graves we left along that trail overwhelmed me. "'Tis nae as easy as it sounds."

"Och," Robert snorted. "The elders will take us tae Puerto Santa Cruz."

Dumbfounded, I snapped out of my memories and Pepe's 'Go' message returned. "But how can they do that?"

Robert gave me an adolescent-like mocking smile as though I'd just asked the dumbest question he'd heard all day. "'Tis but a trifle, Faither. Pay nae mind to how it is done." His smile gave way to a serious look. "The devil ye mention has more tae do with yer fears than the few

199

sticks and stones separating us from our destination."

I had no argument to counter Robert's confidence, only experience. It was impossible to verify an estimation, but I guessed Puerto Santa Cruz was at least one hundred miles distant. Since my arrival on that horrible day when Henry was murdered, I had not tried to ascertain where I had been taken. My wanderings for edibles were confined to a valley of some sort, nestled below high crags, presumably west of the coastal plane.

"I must leave ye for a short time," Robert told me one evening after a lesson on European monarchs.

The unexpected comment caught me by surprise. "Why, and for how long?"

Robert avoided my questioning gaze and looked skyward. "The elders," he said softly. "The time tae leave comes soon." He rocked back on his heels, his furrowed brow revealed concern. "The elders will tell me when."

"Will I also be told?" As dubious as I felt, I had to admit the timing was fortuitous. If we were to secure a passage, we had a better chance if we got to Puerto Santa Cruz now, just before the sailing season began in earnest.

"Ye needn't worry, Faither. Ye will be with me when the time comes."

That night I tossed in my bed unable to sleep. A feeling of foreboding consumed me. Something significant was about to happen. Something that would change the course of my life and the life of my son. I could only hope for the better.

It didn't surprise me when, the next morning after Pepe served me my breakfast tea, Robert appeared in my chambers just as Pepe was leaving. The two hesitated at the door's threshold and I realized it was the first time I knew Robert to be in close company with his biological faither. No audible words were spoken, and no expression escaped their faces, but I sensed a quick moment of reckoning. The giants shun expressions of emotion, yet I suspect their raw and unvarnished emotions can't be completely ignored or controlled any more than mine can. I could only hope they appreciated one another. Once Pepe left, Robert turned his attention toward me. He looked animated, his eyes brighter than usual, his face flushed, almost glowing. His message was clear without a word being said and I followed Robert out the door.

"Isn't there some ceremony?" I asked. "Announcing our departure?"

Robert shook his head. "There is nae departure in the elders' world. They be always near."

We were moving too fast to discuss the subtleties of 'near', so I dropped the subject and obediently followed Robert as he trotted through a maze of corridors. An opening led to a grassy area, open to the sky. Two giants stood in the middle of the area, each one equipped with a rudimentary saddle made of woven fabric and cordage strapped to their back.

"They will take us," Robert said. With little effort, my boy lifted me into the saddle and roped me in. Even though he be a wee boy o but two years, he was noo near my shoulder in height. "Do nae be afraid," he added when he was done.

"I will be brave," I said while recollections of my last journey when Henry died filled my mind with dread. Once again giving my life up to God's will, I sunk my head into the thick matted hair of my giant conveyance, shut my eyes, and accepted my fate.

The sensation was like being aboard a ship in rough seas. I could not see our progress, but I could feel the giant's muscles rolling from side to side as it used all four appendages to propel us along a route accented by the scent of alpine foliage and cool temperatures. I surmised we were following the cordillera's ridgeline. At times the rolling stopped, and I sensed we were close to flying, or perhaps falling. Either way, the giant never wavered, and his confidence gave me confidence as well.

The journey ended abruptly, just as I felt myself falling asleep. The sudden loss of movement jarred me awake and Robert's hands were upon me untying the saddle's cords. "We walk noo," Robert said. "The town is near." It took me a minute to get my bearings and during that time the two giants ascended a high outcropping and disappeared into the gathering shadows.

"I am in yer world now," Robert said. He gazed at the twinkling glow of Puerto Santa Cruz spread out below us. As we took our first steps, Robert's upright posture changed to a crouch and his expression appeared anxious, as if he was approaching danger.

"Stand tall," I admonished him. "This is yer world as well. Ye might as well face it with a grin."

We looked to be an odd pair as we walked through the outlying district. Robert was dressed in crudely altered remnants of Elizabeth's garments, and I was wearing the repeatedly mended outfit that Manuel so generously supplied me with. I suppose we looked like vagabonds, which to all intents we were. Nobody cared, however, since the inhabitants of Puerto Santa Cruz we saw looked to be errant vagabonds themselves, intent on making their way to destinies near and far. We had arrived late in the afternoon in the month of September, early spring, at the beginning of a stormy night, rain mixed with sleet stinging our faces as we searched for shelter.

Wide-eyed, Robert gave up his initial apprehension

and didn't hide his astonishment observing the novel particulars of a rough-hewn frontier town. Ramshackle hovels lined both sides of the muddy street, some with faint, flickering light emanating through sealskin-covered windows. Vehicles of all shapes and sizes drawn by every conceivable draught animal competed for headway amid a babble of indecipherable Spanish and local languages. We said little as we tried to make sense of our destination and our future.

Robert was chilled and shivering when I finally secured us lodging in a cramped and stuffy public room near the harbor. A crude wood stove at one end of the room glowed red, giving the place a modicum of warmth in the dim light. Robert sat opposite me, each of us huddled under a thin blanket atop straw mattresses. A chorus of snores, coughs, and muttering accompanied our conversation. "Get some sleep," I told him. "Tomorrow will be a busy day."

Robert nodded but didn't move. "Something is nae right," he muttered. Both his hands pressed against his temples. "My head is hurting." He squeezed his eyes shut and sneezed uncontrollably for the first time in his life. It was an ominous, disheartening sound that sent a chill down my spine.

"God bless ye," I said without thinking, and I gave him my kerchief. I tried to act nonchalant, but my concern must have been apparent, for Robert's face was flushed with fever and fear. "God bless ye?" he replied, rubbing his red nose. "Am I tae regard yer blessing as a plea for intervention by a power greater than yerself?" Caught in the dim light, beads of sweat glistened across Robert's brow. "Is my condition grave?"

I draped my blanket across his shoulders. "Never mind my comment. I suspect ye be suffering from a malady called influenza. 'Tis a sickness also sometimes called ague. The symptoms are most uncomfortable, but nae usually lethal if ye rest and stay warm." I gently pressed Robert back on the mattress and covered him with both our blankets. "Ye be young and strong." I took the kerchief and wiped his face. "But ye need tae rest."

I stood and buttoned my coat up to my chin. "I will make some inquiries and return shortly. Hopefully, I will bring back some good news."

Robert reached for me, and we held hands. His felt cold and clammy. "Fear nae, son," I said and squeezed his hand. "The influenza is loathsome misery, but 'tis temporary. Ye shall recover soon."

When I returned a few hours later, Robert was sleeping so soundly I checked his pulse to make sure he remained among the living. I prayed his unnatural biological heritage of man and beast would be strong enough to withstand the ravages of the ague. "Rest easy, my son," I whispered. "A ship will arrive soon."

Three days later, Robert removed the blankets and raised himself to a sitting position. Weak sunlight streamed into the room through gaps in the walls and roof. The disturbance woke me from a nap, and, regaining my bearings, I moved to the foot of Robert's mattress. Robert's pale complexion and dark, sunken eyes worried me, but the fever had passed and he regarded me with an alert sense of presence. I nodded and smiled. "I have good news," I said.

Robert frowned and crossed his arms over his chest. "I hungry."

"I am glad to hear it." I suppressed my good news and foraged through my satchel for the pieces of bread and strips of smoked fish fillets I had saved for him. His incorrect grammar usage surprised me, but I ignored the mistake and blamed it on the ague. He studied my offering closely, then ate the bread without comment. "Don't worry," I assured him, "it may look and taste strange, but 'tis perfectly fine. I'll fetch ye some hot broth tae wash it down."

When I returned, Robert was sitting on the mattress with his feet on the floor; across from him, a wizened old rotter jabbered away in Spanish. The fish fillets were scattered on the floor, uneaten.

"Kin ye unnerstan anything he's saying?" I sat on

the edge of Robert's bunk and handed him a steaming beaker of chicken broth.

"I want home," he replied. "Home." His dull eyes turned toward the door. "Go. Go home." His body shook with the advent of another sneezing fit. I gave him my kerchief but he brushed it away, his face a torment of anguish, mucus, and spittle.

"What is the matter, Robert? We are going to Europe. Remember?" I gently moved his hand, holding the beaker toward his mouth.

He took a deep breath and drank. "Ye said Europe good place." He finished the broth in two gulps, handed me the beaker, and laid back down. "Civilization, culture, science, good things."

"That is correct," I replied, relieved to hear him use better English. I assumed the broth was reenergizing him. "Ye will find happiness there."

Robert sneezed and closed his eyes. "Sickness, filth, ugliness!" He opened his eyes and waved his arm. "Ye told me nothing of this! Why secret?"

I stood, distancing myself from Robert's wrath and rubbed my chin. "I dinnae keep those things a secret, Robert. I forgot about them. I've been away from home for over five years and my memory gets selective over time. The bad things fade oot first." I touched his shoulder and pulled our blankets over his chest. His breathing slowed. "I be sorry for omitting sickness, filth, and ugliness in our talks," I continued at a whisper. "'Twas an honest oversight."

He was sound asleep before I finished my apology. I kept the rum in his broth a secret, but I thought it was a prudent strategy. No amount of persuasion could do as well. Persuasion was not going to ease my anxiety about Robert's symptoms, either. Was the ague affecting him in a peculiar way due to his unusual biological makeup? Might there be debilitating side effects? What if he was severely incapacitated?

I eased my agitated mind by going over what I had learned earlier this morning. The harbormaster had informed me a merchantman was due to arrive in a week's time, and when I explained my circumstances and where I was from, he told me a ship had departed for Edinburgh some four years ago. He couldn't remember exactly when, but it was early summer.

When I pressed him for more information, he remembered a high official from the Crown had made inquiries about our expedition. The official's name was withheld. The harbormaster added that the ship departed without ceremony after a lengthy search uncovered no sign. The news brought me back to the longboat that passed us on the river at Bahia San Julian. Had it been searching for us? Is it possible that high official was Lord Monboddo? After killing our captain, Peter would never show his face in Edinburgh again, so the dearth of news might have goaded him into action.

Robert stirred. He turned over on his side, facing me, and opened his eyes. "Have ye good news?"

"Aye. A ship arrives in a week's time. It will take on supplies, destined for Le Havre, France. I aim tae get us aboard."

"The elders willna take me back," Robert moaned. "I have nae home, so I follow ye." He sat up, his eyes watering. "More broth."

Another long swallow precipitated an uncontrolled sneezing and coughing fit. The older man from the next cot gasped and crossed himself. "Dios Mio," he exclaimed. "La plaga!" He pulled a flask from a pocket, took a long gulp, then got on his unsteady feet and staggered out the door. "Ándale! Ándale!" His hoarse, gravelly voice echoed from outside. "La plaga!" Some heads lifted off their pillows from nearby mattresses then dropped back when the commotion subsided.

Robert lay back down and closed his eyes. "Give me blankets." He closed his eyes once I covered him. "Rest. Rest and warmth...." He was sound asleep before I left his side.

The merchantman Ariadne arrived two weeks later in wind-tossed seas that slowed the resupply work by an additional week. I hoped the extra time would be to our benefit, as Robert's health remained a worrisome unknown. He had good days when he seemed his old self, but he always relapsed into feverish delirium in the later afternoon. At least the serious setback he had during the first days seemed to be over. I tried to keep him sheltered, out of the wind, but when he had a mind to break away from his confinement, there was no stopping him until he returned weak and exhausted. Having witnessed the ravages it had inflicted on my homeland, I knew influenza was nothing to take lightly. All I could do was hope his unnatural biological condition would influence his affliction in a positive manner.

Alas, our departure date coincided with a setback, and Robert woke up that morning tormented with fever and headache. "Ye must marshal yer strength and hide any appearance o illness for a few hours until the ship has set sail," I told him while we dressed and packed our few belongings. "Keep yer head down and avoid eye contact when greeting the captain. Once we be oot tae sea, he willna turn back."

Robert shivered. "Canna we ask for special consideration?" He coughed once, then again, the second ending with a gasp. "I loath tae risk everything on a pretense."

I shook my head. "The captain will never knowingly endanger his ship by allowing a sick passenger tae board." I hefted my satchel over my shoulder to close the discussion. "We either avoid detection, or we don't board. 'Tis nae room for negotiation or bribery." I laughed. "If we even had the means tae bribe. We were lucky they had room for us, but I had tae promise I'd pay for our passage when we arrived in France. The good Lord only knows how that will play out."

Robert took a deep breath. "I will do my best, Faither. I must nae show weakness."

"Right," I replied. "Stand straight and step lively. Smile, but don't talk unless yer addressed. If someone inquires about yer condition, tell them ye suffer from allergies and say nae more." I clutched Robert's shoulder. "The secret tae avoiding detection is tae disappear."

Robert rewarded me with a rare smile. "Ye often say the strangest things, Faither."

A line of workmen carrying parcels appeared out of the misty morning when we approached the Ariadne tied up at the dock. A gangway was rigged from the dock leading to the Ariadne's main deck and men filed up the gangway where an officer stood watching the procession. I pointed at the uniformed sailor. "See how quickly he handles the loading? He wants tae get everything and everyone on board quickly and set sail before the ebb tide turns. A brief hello and our names are all he wants." Behind us, the line was already filling out with grunting men handling heavy loads. Robert's red, runny eyes and nose filled me with dread, and I mumbled a little prayer the sailor would be too distracted to notice. "Make eye contact and nod approval when I speak, but say nothing," I whispered, more for my benefit than his.

Robert smothered a sneeze with my kerchief. "I will do as ye say."

"Stand straight, noo. Look lively," I reiterated, flashing a hopeful smile of encouragement.

The first mate was signing a document when we reached the top of the gangway. "Where the bleeding hell is that quartermaster?" he shouted at a young man standing nervously at his side. "Damn his eyes. You, Clive. Go find Branson and bring him around. I need his signature."

As the boy scurried off, I saw my chance. "John Hempstead and son Robert boarding as passengers," I announced with a cheery voice, standing between the sailor and Robert.

"Make it quick, Clive. We don't have all day!" the first mate replied.

The first mate twisted around and eyed me with an

impatient look. "Bloody passengers." He opened a portfolio and glanced at a manifest. "Hempstead, father and son, bound for Southampton by way of Le Havre." Behind us, the workmen grunted their impatience.

"Right." I acknowledged the first mate with a nod. "Which way tae our quarters?" I felt Robert stiffen behind me. I prayed he wouldn't sneeze.

The first mate eyed me with a suspicious grimace then, without bothering to appraise Robert, pointed to a portside gangway that led below deck. "Take that below," he grumbled. "A seaman will show you your berths."

Robert took a step away from the first mate and turned his head toward the ship's bow.

"Wait a minute!" The first mate roared.

We both froze in our tracks and didn't turn around.

"You're to stay in your quarters until you hear the all-clear signal. Is that understood?"

"Aye, sir," Robert and I both answered.

"I don't want to see passengers gallivanting on deck and getting in the way while we're loading."

"We will stay below, sir," I replied. "Until the all-clear signal is called."

Robert remained quiet until we reached an open area below deck where we were told we could procure hammocks. Empty hammocks swung about listlessly, attached to vertical posts. Robert felt a hammock's rough canvas texture and gave me a quizzical look. "What is this?"

"'Tis a sailor's bed," I replied. "Welcome tae life at sea." And for a few hilarious moments, I instructed Robert in the fine art of settling oneself in the obstinate contraption.

The brief release from the tension of boarding was soon over when three other passengers, all of them older men, claimed their hammocks. After introductions were made, our group settled into private pursuits, reading, napping, and waiting for the all-clear signal. Robert stifled a sneeze, which seemed to go unnoticed, but I silently prayed it would be his last.

After a fitful nap, I was awakened by coughing. I sensed from the repeated rolling motion we were experiencing that the Ariadne was underway. Robert was sitting awake in his hammock covering his face with my kerchief.

A passenger hopped out of his hammock just as a high-pitched whistle sounded. "I trust that was the all-clear signal?" Over his shoulder he said, "I say, that is a worrisome cough you have there, sir. Are you quite all right?" He kept his distance and headed toward the gangway.

Robert nodded as the gentleman passed and blew

214

his nose. "Pardon. Allergies. Something stored in hold, nae doot."

"He's always been sensitive tae harmful vapors," I added. "Ever since he was a wee laddie. I blame it on his mother; God rest her soul."

The passenger gave a quick nod and held his scarf over his face. "Most unfortunate," he grumbled.

After he left, Robert smothered another sneeze.

The afternoon sun, now close to the horizon, streamed through an open hatch. I worried about Robert's tendency to relapse in the later afternoon hours. It would not bode us well if Robert's first impressions with the ship's crew and passengers were that of sneezing and coughing. "Rest now," I replied. "I'm going to go topside and survey our new home. I will bring ye back something tae eat from the galley, err, I mean scullery."

The walk renewed my strength and rekindled my resolve to fulfill Elizabeth's ambitious undertaking. Keeping close to the bulwark, I let my mind wander as the ship's crew scurried by; the vast Atlantic rolled out to the darkening horizon. It was all left up to me. Four dead, six counting our captain and his first mate. Five years of suffering, isolation, and privation left me with the prize at hand. A giant – alive and cogent – ready to fulfill the destinies of his forebearers and his own future.

All I had to do now was get him in touch with the European scientific societies in one piece. It seemed easy at this point, after all I'd been through, but I knew better.

I was on my way aft from the forecastle when I was approached by a formally dressed gentleman wearing a long coat, spectacles, and buckle shoes. "Excuse me, sir. Are you Mister Hempstead?" He gave me a slight bow and an enquiring look over the top of his spectacles.

"Aye, sir. I am."

"I am Doctor Clark, the ship's surgeon. If you don't mind, I wish to speak to you about your son, Robert Hempstead, I presume?"

I did my best to suppress my surprise. "Aye, Robert is my son. Is there something amiss?"

Doctor Clark gestured for us to repair to a sheltered corner on the quarterdeck. He spoke in a low tone. "I regret to inform you, sir, but your son is quite ill. He shows symptoms consistent with what we know to be the very contagious fever called influenza. Are you aware of his condition?"

I took a breath and stuck to my story, hoping Robert did the same. "He has been sneezing since we came on board, but we assumed he was suffering from allergies, nothing more."

The doctor dropped his eyes to the deck. "Indeed. Be that as it may, we have taken the utmost of caution and have removed him from the passengers' quarters and, for the sake of our crew and passengers' safety, remanded him to the ship's hold until further notice."

I grabbed a stanchion to keep my balance and steadied myself, my mind reeling. Robert forcefully pulled from his bed by strangers and conducted to the cold, wet confines of the ship's hold? Good God, he'll die down there. I wanted to run to his aid, but I knew a desperate move would not improve matters. "Surely ye canna mean tae leave him there," I said. "With all due respect, sir. He has a rather delicate constitution."

The doctor snorted. "He is young, and if he's only suffering from allergies, as you say, they will clear up in due time." He cocked an eyebrow. "I have noted in my incident report to the captain that your son's symptoms came upon him quite suddenly." With a stern look, the doctor raised his voice. "Following his admission aboard, having shown no symptoms at that time we departed. Do you agree?" He removed a sheet of paper from his coat pocket.

I backed away a step, wishing to run to my son's comfort. "What's this?"

Doctor Clark held up what looked like a writ of some sort. "'Tis an order of confinement. Your son will remain isolated until such a time that I find he is to be no longer a threat and ready to return to the ship's company." He placed the paper in my hand. "Please read this, sir."

Overcome with anxiety, I paid little attention to the words. "When can I visit him?" was all I could think to say.

Doctor Clark removed the paper from my hands and shook his head. "It states clearly in the order, Mister Hempstead, there shall be no visitation, except for medical purposes, while the patient is confined." He returned the paper to his coat pocket. "We must take every precaution. If, by chance, your son has the influenza," he gave me a stern look, "I fear the fever could spread throughout the ship's close conditions like wildfire."

"But Doctor, why canna —"

"There are no exceptions, sir." With that, Doctor Clark turned to leave. "Mind, if you attempt entry, you will find yourself confined to the brig. Now good day, sir." With that, he proceeded toward the stern without another word.

Could I talk to Robert through the closed door? Can we still communicate telepathically? My mind raced as I stood, too shocked to move. I listened for his voice in my head, but all I heard was the empty echo of my vexation.

There was no guard at the door leading to the ship's hold, but it was barred and padlocked. It was late, past midnight, and the few sounds I could discern in the background were muted and infrequent. Orders from some officer followed by a seaman's acknowledgment, announcements of time and watch change, and the low rumble of snores coming from the passenger's quarters directly overhead. I put my ear to the door and heard nothing. "Robert!" I whispered.

A long wait later, a shuffling sound came, and my head erupted with a painful squeal. Nonsense sounds emanated from behind the door. "Robert," I repeated a little louder this time. "'Tis me, yer faither."

"I willna live long," came Robert's reply. "Elders are grieving. We are lost." His last words were interrupted by coughing.

"Save yer strength, son." I held my breath when one of the snorers broke his pattern and sputtered. "Concentrate on the love yer elders and I have for ye." Tears filled my eyes following another fusillade of coughing. "Yer life is precious. Dinnae waste it."

The next evening, while at dinner, a sailor handed me a letter and quickly removed himself before I could ask about its origin or intention. My name was written boldly across the envelope.

Curious eyes skittered around me as I opened the letter.

"Dear, sir," it began. "It is with the utmost sadness

that I have the duty as Captain of the merchant ship Ariadne to inform you of your son's demise. Doctor Clark confirmed the patient succumbed to the effects of the influenza fever. The time of death is considered to be sometime during the afternoon watch. We will attend to his burial at sea promptly at four bells without ceremony. You may participate as a witness. If there is any consolation, sir, it is that the fever was kept in check and did not contaminate the ship's crew or passengers. May God have mercy on his soul.

Your obedient servant, Reginald Cox, Captain."

My son, wrapped unceremoniously in a canvas shroud, slipped off the rail of the Ariadne and hit the water with hardly a sound. Beyond my tears, my whole body roared with grief for my lost son and shame for having failed our mission. Standing alone, after the brief ceremony, I was overcome by my anguish and collapsed. I wondered why the world didn't end. Why hadn't the giants howled in rage from across the horizon and killed me for my ineptitude? All I could do in repentance was follow my son. I crawled toward the rail, but hands grabbed me before reaching my goal, and I lost consciousness when a blow to my head ended my struggles.

Smelling salts brought me around, and now lying in

my hammock, I stared into the bespectacled, questioning eyes of Doctor Clark. It was all I could do to restrain myself from ripping off his spectacles and spitting in his face.

"He wasn't your son, was he," Clark said.

"What do ye care whose son he was?"

"Because I did an autopsy, postmortem."

"Och, so?"

"A most unusual case. In front of my very eyes, the boy, or thing, disintegrated. No blood, nor flesh, nor bone. The moment I put a scalpel to its chest, it turned from physical form to a gray mist that hung in the air then dissipated out the porthole." Clark stared at me wide-eyed. "I wrapped the shroud around ballast rocks so as not to frighten the men. Who or what was this creature?"

I let go of my grief and exhaled a breath of relief. Robert was dead, but the knowledge of his existence did not die with him. A witness in the physical world verified the giants' existence, no matter how dubious the verification may be. Doctor Clark acknowledged the unexplainable. That was all I had to bring home.

"He was a giant," I said. "The last o his kind."

Chapter Eleven

I arrived in Edinburgh's Leith Docks on a bitterly cold November afternoon, 1756. It was six years ago we left that October afternoon with streamers flying and bands playing at the edge of Leith Docks. I brought back nothing but the clothes I was provided by the crew whose ship brought me from France. No one was waiting for me, and I was penniless. My only recourse was to make my way to the King's Arms and hope I might recognize a familiar face.

My walk from the Docks along Leith Walk to Constitution Street, then to Bernard Street, took me past familiar promenades, coffee houses, shops and stalls, and crowded doorways. Despite the chill, the town

seemed livelier, busier than when I left it, although the
noise and stench were the same. The scent of tobacco and
filth from the street filled my nose. Some new
developments – such as a theatre house and a
haberdashers – disoriented me, but I found my way. My
pace was slower than those who passed me, and I was
ignored by the bustling crowd and throngs of hackneys,
coaches, and chairmen that choked the thoroughfare. It
made me realize how transitory we are, how quickly we
are forgotten. How I missed Robert and my colleagues.
It was as if I'd come back from the dead, which in some
ways I had.

The Kings Arms was as I remembered it. My friend
William Purdy welcomed me into the quiet taproom
with a cheery hello and a "where have ye been" while
drawing a pint of my favorite bitters. He joined me at a
table and waved off my apologies for not paying. "Ye
been gone so long, John. There must be a story tae tell,"
he replied. "And if 'tis good enough, maybe I will
consider it fair compensation."

The pub was empty, but as opening time came, the
crowd appeared, and I recognized some faces. Other
people gathered around as I told William my story of
shipwreck, death, discovery, and abandonment. The
enquiring looks on people's faces gave me pause. I felt
more like a curiosity than the unfortunate survivor of a

scientific expedition, and when I came to the part about Elizabeth and our son, I equivocated. I did not stray far from the truth, but I left Robert out of my story along with the bits I felt might be regarded as more salacious than scientifically important for this audience. Still, the confusing invention I hastily cribbed together about Elizabeth and her newborn son's tragic deaths in the company of giant apes elicited gasps and mutterings of astonishment. I hope Roger will forgive my lie when I insinuated that he was the alleged faither.

I was sure Elizabeth would not have hesitated to disclose every detail of Robert's birth, but I did not feel at liberty to share those painful memories with strangers. I was plied with food and drink until I finished at the sound of the closing bell. The crowd sat stunned, in stony silence, and I waited for absolution or condemnation; I didn't know which I deserved more.

"That is indeed a story," William said as the crowd of listeners chattered amongst themselves. Murmurings of 'hogwash,' 'balderdash,' and 'blasphemy' emanated from the mouths of skeptical faces. William frowned. "If I didnae know ye better, I'd believe it was the rantings of a madman and I'd be tempted to call a constable."

I nodded. "It would seem so, having no means tae substantiate my assertions." I looked around the table. "And ye have every right tae scoff." William was right;

the only thing that stood between me and debtors' prison was a discreditable story with no substance or basis of fact. I shook my head ruefully at the ignominy of my situation. After all we'd been through, for it to come down to this.

"On the other hand," William continued, "nae madman has the imagination tae envision a tale as improbable as yers." He stood. "Time, gentleman!" he commanded. "Our entertainment is over." With a wink, he gestured for me to remain in my seat. When the pub was empty once again, William returned to his seat. "I know ye tae be a reputable man, John. And in principle, I have nae reason tae doot the veracity o yer extraordinary tale."

I sighed and gazed at my empty pint glass. "Thank ye, William. 'Tis most generous o ye."

William pushed the chair back from the table. "I remember yer departure with Elizabeth Burnett and yer four colleagues tae search for the mysterious giant apes." He pulled his pipe out of his pocket and struck a match. "A grand spectacle as I recall. And now ye say brigands thwarted the expedition, mutineers I should say, before ye reached yer destination."

"Correct," I replied. "As I said, Peter, the first mate, and his followers killed our captain and cast our expedition adrift in a longboat."

"Interesting...." William took a puff. "And ye be the lone survivor. Do ye have any idea regarding the whereabouts o yer ship, the Cumberland?" When I shook my head and gave him a blank look, he leaned forward, a stern look upon his face. "Ye left oot Lord Monboddo's rescue attempt. Ye must be aware o Lord Monboddo's rescue voyage, aye?"

The longboat on the river flashed across my memory again. I had left that incident out of my story because it seemed inconsequential. I squirmed in my seat, uncomfortable with William's cross-examination. I wasn't guilty of anything, yet I felt accused. "Indirectly, aye. The harbormaster at Puerto Santa Cruz told me a ship bound for Edinburgh made a stop four years before I arrived."

"And?" William's eyebrows raised.

"The harbormaster told me an official from the Crown was aboard, and a search had been carried oot, for whom he didnae say. He didnae give me the official's name but said the search had been unsuccessful. Sadly, at the time, we were many miles north, near an abandoned outpost called Puerto San Julián."

"How unfortunate."

"Indeed. I wish I could have been there...." I paused. A tear ran down my cheek. "With Elizabeth ... with everyone."

William stood. "The Cumberland never returned, nor has there been any sight o her. That gives credence tae yer account o a mutiny. And I'll take yer word about the missed opportunity at Puerto Santa Cruz." He stepped tae the bar. "But the rest o yer story; the cannibals, the giants, and Elizabeth?" He shook his head. "I would be keeping quiet about all that."

I got to my feet as well, ready to take my leave. "I have nae intention o capitalizing on my colleague's misadventures, William." I donned what little protection my tattered hat and coat provided. I had no destination. Home and Mary were a day's ride and I had only my pride to sustain me. "In the name o science, I only hope tae share my discoveries o native flora with the University's botanical staff."

William waved for me to stop. "I have a free room, John. Stay the night." He smiled. "Ye have earned a night's lodging with the extra drink and victuals yer admiring crowd consumed tonight." He winked, acknowledging the sarcasm of his remark and I smiled back.

I accepted William's favor, but before he escorted me up the stairs, he touched my shoulder. "Mark my word, John, Lord Monboddo will get wind of yer stories. And I daresay he willna waste time tracking ye down." We stopped at the landing, and I felt a shroud of weariness overcome me. "Ye should prepare yourself tae face a furious man, his head full o lurid stories about his daughter fraternizing with beasts, against the laws o God and nature."

Why had I disclosed the story o Elizabeth's death while giving birth? I wondered from the comfort of William's soft bed. *I could have easily said she died o food poisoning, which wouldn't have been far from the truth.*

It seemed I was cursed, to be chased by lies and falsehoods for the remainder of my days. My only hope was that Mary would be there to comfort me during the tribulations that were sure to come. I felt ashamed for the thoughts I once harbored about my wife while I laid in Henry's arms. As my eyes grew heavy, I remembered her love. I remembered everything.

The next day I found a ride home, with the charity of a greengrocer, in the bed of his produce wagon. I expected there'd be some changes; Mary was always looking for ways to improve things, but I was surprised to see the house had been whitewashed, there were new curtains in the windows and a freshly tilled vegetable patch lay barren in the front garden. I was particularly surprised by the vegetable patch since Mary hated gardening work. We often laughed at our contrasting proclivities, me a botanist and she with her black thumb. Had she turned over a new leaf? I smiled at my word play while approaching the door. I only wished I had a bouquet to offer as a gesture of greeting.

"May I help ye, sir?" A young boy stuck his head outside the door before I reached the threshold.

I stopped in my tracks. "I say there, young lad. And who might ye be?"

"My name is Timothy Martin, sir. At yer service."

A women's head appeared above Timothy's. She was much younger than Mary. Before I could say anything, she opened the door and faced me with an inquiring look. "Good day, sir. Are ye looking for someone?"

"Aye, thank ye, madam. I be looking for the mistress o the house, Missus Mary Hempstead."

The woman's expression changed from inquisitive to concern. Her eyes opened wide, and she pushed the boy away from the door. "Och, dear me. Have ye nae heard?"

I removed my hat. "Heard what, pray tell." It was getting difficult to keep my balance. My knees were shaking.

"Aboot Missus Hempstead's passing. I'm so sorry, but she died o the influenza. It would be six months ago noo. Her husband...." She hesitated when I staggered backward, struggling to stay upright. Stepping outside the door, the woman approached me. "Gracious me, are ye Mister Hempstead?"

"Indeed, I am, madam." I willed myself not to fall. "I was nae aware o my wife's demise. I've just returned...." I let out an uncontrollable sob. "I've just noo returned from a long voyage."

The woman took my hand, her face ashen. "God save us. How terrible! Please, Mister Hempstead. Please, come inside."

Under the dire circumstances of learning about my wife's death, I could barely keep up with Missus Martin's story. I sat, dumbfounded, and drank tea. I had no desire to contest ownership, the house had been taken from me, not by man, but by the hand of God. Its furnishings and adornments were unfamiliar to me, reflecting the lives of strangers. I could only reply to Missus Martin's queries with grunts.

What was to become of me now? An old, broken man with no means to support himself and no family to come to his aid. All I had was a story. A story that had already been vilified as an unbelievable fantasy and a blasphemous insult to a famous family member. When Mister Martin arrived, and with nowhere to turn, I humbly accepted Missus and Mister Martin's gracious invitation to share young Timothy's room until such a time as I could find a future.

Henry appeared to me that night as I slept in

Timothy's bed. There was no interaction, just Henry standing in front of me, smiling. I smiled back and felt an unusual sense of freedom. I'd lost everything, my old familiar life was gone, yet I was not afraid. I felt like doors opened to opportunities unknown to me in my past.

During breakfast, Sean, Mister Martin, informed me he worked at King James College. Not as a faculty member, mind, but on the support staff. "I be a glorified domestic," he called it. "Picking up after those thoughtless entitled brats."

"I'm familiar with those ruffians," I replied. "I was once employed as a clerk in botanic studies."

Thankfully, the Martin's didn't pry about my experiences, and when I told them about my voyage, they only mentioned hearing snippets of news, nothing more. "Means nothing tae us," noted Missus Martin. "Begging yer pardon, but the goings-on o rich intellectuals puts nae food on our table."

I assured them I was not a rich intellectual and they were satisfied I had merely played a minor, supportive role in the expedition, which suited me fine.

"Would ye care tae accompany me tae the College?" Sean asked while Missus Martin cleared the table and got Timothy ready for school.

"I would indeed," I replied. "It would be a tonic tae

see my old haunts and perhaps meet with a few chaps."

I felt like a stranger in a familiar place, walking the halls of King's College. I expected to be approached by a bailiff and escorted off at any minute. As luck would have it, I eluded the constabulary and entered the offices of botanic sciences without mishap. Somebody was sitting at my old work carrel. He looked familiar, but I could not place him. Perhaps it was more a similarity than a recognition. About my age and size, he smiled and held out a hand. "Good day, sir." He had a friendly, congenial voice that immediately disarmed me. "Be ye looking for someone in botanic sciences?"

Looking to my right and left, I took his hand and smiled back. "I'm a past member o the botanic science laboratory, John Hempstead."

"Aye, I recognize the name. Ye be quite well kent around here, Mister Hempstead; at least yer absence has been well kent. Welcome home, and I be pleased tae make yer acquaintance. Ewan Kavanagh at yer service."

The warmth of Ewan's welcome was a balm on my agitated feelings, and I felt immediately at ease. Then, out of the corner of my eye, I spied my friend Cranston. "Aye, there is someone," I said, raising my voice. "Brian Cranston. He might remember me."

Brian looked in my direction. "John! John

Hempstead! Yer back!"

Three more heads appeared from behind partitions.

"We had given ye up for dead!"

"Where's Roger?"

"Is Jacob with ye?"

"Did ye find the giants?"

A shiver of anxiety ran up my spine as my colleagues gathered 'round.

"And Elizabeth," someone added. "Lord Monboddo has nae been the same since he returned from his voyage o rescue. Is Elizabeth here with ye?"

"Sadly, she is nae," I opened. Thus began an obligatory explanation of my absence. I tried to concentrate on the key points and focus more on my botanical discoveries. Still, it didn't take long before I grew weary from fielding all the lurid queries, comments about the deaths of the expedition members, and news about the giants. When I described Elizabeth's death, I remembered Henry's presence last night. I stuck to my original story, generalizing about the tragedy of Elizabeth's miscarriage and death in the company of giant apes. There was some unsolicited commentary when I continued my lie about Roger being the faither.

I was describing my discoveries of eatable flora when there came a crashing sound and the stomping of feet that echoed through the outer gallery. "Where is that insufferable cad!" came a strident voice. My blood ran cold. It was the unmistakable voice of Lord Monboddo.

His retinue had to restrain him when he saw me, his face red with anger. "How dare ye insinuate my daughter's death came about in the company o wild animals!" he sputtered. "Unhand me!" he shouted. "I want tae thrash this scoundrel with my bare hands!"

The violent intrusion caught me off-guard, and I froze in the company of my colleagues. All I could do was stare at the enraged man. "Nae." I finally summoned the strength to speak. "She was unable tae help herself. The giants merely witnessed her death."

"Ye be a liar!" Monboddo roared. "My daughter may have died, may she rest in peace, but she most certainly wouldn't have allowed her distress tae be shared in the company o a troupe of overgrown baboons! How dare ye slander my dearly departed Elizabeth's reputation with such a monstrous fabrication! I demand ye retract yer lies!"

In the wake of Monboddo's rage, I prepared to take Elizabeth's story to my grave, which seemed imminent by the looks of him. Elizabeth did not deserve the repercussions that would come from disclosing what happened. Nae. Better to sugar-coat reality with fairytales so my esteemed and learned countryman could sleep at night. "I be nae a liar, sir." I boldly replied.

Henry's smile came into focus behind my thoughts. *Except when expedient, John,* he whispered. "But the full account o Elizabeth's discoveries and her tragic end will wait to be heard another day."

"Dinnae ye hold back on me!" Monboddo fumed. "I want the truth!" He raised his fist. "If ye dinnae talk, I will have ye arrested on the charge o perjury and defamation o character!"

I took a step toward Monboddo. A newfound inner strength propelled me to counter Monboddo's threat, but before I could respond, Mister Kavanagh interrupted.

"I assume, sir, ye be referring tae Mister Hempstead's account o his experiences told last night at the King's Arms." Monboddo paused, taken by surprise. "And if that is so," Ewan continued, "yer accusations are nae based on an accurate account."

Monboddo shrugged away from the grip holding him in check. "I have it on the authority of *three* eyewitnesses! They all say Mr. Hempstead defamed my beloved daughter in the worst possible manner!" He glowered and pointed at me. "I demand immediate redress o this grave offense!"

Ewan cleared his throat. "There was another eyewitness," he said. "*I* was at the King's Arms last night and heard Mister Hempstead's story as well."

The group looked at one another in bewilderment,

me included. *Is that why Ewan looks familiar?* I wondered.

For a rare moment, Lord Monboddo fell silent.

"I can easily understand the misinterpretation under the circumstances," Ewan said. "There was much alcohol consumed, and John's words were difficult tae follow in the pub's tumult. People were nae paying attention. I can imagine how easily Mister Hempstead's discussion about Elizabeth's company with giants could be construed as something more ... lurid and entertaining, ye might say ... than the truth."

Lord Monboddo finally found his voice. "Whyfore did ye kept quiet until noo?"

Heads nodded. It was a fair question. I wondered myself.

"Because I had nae met Mister Hempstead at the time, and I had nae reason tae suspect the man's story was anything more than the ravings o a drunken braggart." Ewan smiled. "I remained in a corner o the public room and minded my business. However, as the story unfolded, I recognized it tae be the one everyone had been discussing for some time. So, I listened more carefully. This morning, I decided tae keep my own counsel, assuming Mister Hempstead would make an appearance."

The color of Lord Monboddo's cheeks lightened. "Ye imply, sir, the men who spoke tae me be liars?"

"Indeed nae, sir. Their interpretation o John's story is merely the result o hasty presumption amid lively banter and crosstalk. More tae the point," Ewan gave me a nod. "I wager the actual story 'tis likely far less entertaining."

A thin smile crossed Lord Monboddo's face. He sat and his stare turned inward. "Tell me, Hempstead. Tell me what happened tae my daughter."

I took a seat across from him. The others removed themselves, leaving us alone. For a moment I collected my thoughts, weighing fact against fiction. I had told a fabricated version of my story twice in two days' time, and the prospect of telling my fanciful yarn yet again felt disconcerting.

Lord Monboddo eyed me suspiciously.

"Elizabeth discovered a civilization o giants, as described in Pigafetta's journal," I opened. "Despite being subjected tae the most difficult adversities one can imagine, she never wavered from her mission."

"Aye," Lord Monboddo interrupted. "I am nae surprised tae hear about Elizabeth's strong and resolute spirit. And the giants? Well, that remains tae be substantiated." He leaned forward in his chair. "But the assertions about her dying in the company o wild beasts…. " He paused and slapped the table. "However *those* assertions were interpreted, what's the truth in that?"

"The truth is Elizabeth died while giving birth. And 'tis also true, at the time she died, Elizabeth was living in a community o giants, myself included. I call them giants, because they were nae apes, as we ken them. Aside from their size, these giants possessed physical features that were remarkably similar tae our own. As tae whether we were their guests or prisoners, I dinnae ken for sure."

"Go on," Monboddo urged.

I leaned back and closed my eyes, revisiting that horrible event. "I was nae present at the time of her death," I continued. "I was told after the fact that Elizabeth and her bairn did nae survive."

"They spoke tae ye?" Monboddo stared at me, wide-eyed.

"That is correct. Elizabeth had mastered their language quite well. I could only manage a few sentences."

"Preposterous!" Monboddo stood and walked to a window. He stared at the garden outside the offices, his hands behind his back. "Ye mean tae say these apes were civilized, rational creatures?"

I shook my head. "That would require a sustained scientific investigation, sir. From what I could ascertain, the giants' lives were very different from ours. Different customs, different values, different beliefs...." I almost said a different reality, but I refrained for fear of vexing Monboddo even more. "It would be disingenuous to assume anything at this point."

Monboddo did not reply. While he stood with his back to me, I contemplated my next words. *Should I tell him what actually happened tae Elizabeth?* He seemed receptive to the truth, but my unspoken allegation about Roger left me no choice but to maintain the lie. Changing stories now would be more damaging than the truth itself.

Cranston's voice interrupted my thoughts. "It's Sean Martin. He's waiting at the door and wants tae know if ye be accompanying him home."

I breathed a sigh of relief as Monboddo broke his concentration. He frowned at me, but his look was not intimidating. "Come by my house tomorrow," he said. "Ye havnae told me the whole story." He set his calling card on the table in front of me and turned to leave. "Come for tea," he said over his shoulder.

"I'd be honored," I replied as Monboddo, and his retinue marched out of the room. Their clacking heels echoed up and down the gallery. While I made my goodbyes, Ewan stopped next to me and reached across the table for a sheet of stationery, his hand near mine. "We have a new Chancellor," he said.

I rested my hand atop Ewan's while picking up Monboddo's card. "Thank ye, Ewan," I said. A rush of emotion filled my heart. I meant my touch to be an innocent gesture of appreciation, but the touch set off fireworks.

Ewan didn't move. "I was only clarifying a misunderstanding."

We shared a nod, acknowledging Ewan's clarification was only partially true. Somehow, Ewan knew the whole truth lay somewhere else, and he had taken a substantial risk on my behalf.

I savored the feel of Ewan's touch. *'Tis Henry's hand,* I thought. *The very same.*

I removed my hand while Ewan took pen and ink and wrote. "I suggest ye ask for an appointment with Chancellor Wallace," he said, handing me a letter addressed to the Chancellor. "I'd be honored tae facilitate the introduction. I'm sure he'd be interested tae hear about yer discoveries."

After placing the sheet in a pocket, I gathered the courage to look into Ewan's eyes. "I'd be interested in hearing about yern."

End

Author's Note

Thank you for reading my book.

The characters and situations are fictional, but I've tried to instill emotions in the characters that are common to us all. Elizabeth Burnett and her colleagues contend with love, loss, courage, and self-discovery as they cope with the forces of nature, along with the forces within and among themselves.

The inspiration behind *Giants* came from many sources, including historical references to giant beings, such as The Epic of Gilgamesh, along with a 16th century eye-witness account of a giants' sighting.

Were the legendary giants of Bigfoot (N. America), Atlas (Greek), Balor (Ireland), and Goliath (Judeo-Christian) real? Why do they continue to exist in our literature and popular culture even if the alleged remnants of their existence have never been verified? Ecologist Robert Michael Pyle argues that most cultures have humanlike giants in their folk history.

I address these questions with an adventure story that takes place in a strange, unforgiving land, where adversity is the norm and survival is a fleeting illusion.

I sincerely hope you enjoy reading *Giants* as much as I enjoyed writing it.

Acknowledgment

My wife, mentor and patient advisor, Becky; Benicia's Authors' Workshop, and Critique Circle.

I would like to express my heartfelt gratitude to all those who have supported me while researching and writing *Giants*. Your encouragement has been instrumental in bringing this project to fruition.

The beta readers: John Casey, Carol LaHines, and Jim Metzner, enriched the book's content and made it more authentic.

The editors, Pauline Harris, and Penny Dowden of *Between the Lines Publishing*, contributed immensely to every aspect of the *Giants'* story. Their expertise and attention to detail are deeply appreciated.

A special thanks to Abby Macenka and her team at *Between the Lines Publishing* for taking a chance with *Giants* and turning my story into reality.

I extend my appreciation to my friends and colleagues at Critique Circle who provided suggestions and feedback during *Giants'* early days. Thank you for your time and for being a sounding board for my emerging ideas.

As always, thanks to my poet wife, Becky, for your patience and understanding during the highs and lows (especially the lows) during this project.

I hope *Giants* brings to my readers a new perspective about the mysterious 'giant' myth that continues to fascinate cultures world-wide.

Jim is a California-based writer of historical, literary and science fiction. He and his prize-winning poet wife enjoy a small-town lifestyle near the San Francisco Bay area. Jim earned an MA in U.S. History. His professional career has included military service, teaching, research librarian and technical writing. Jim is an active participant in his community's literary organization, serving as a board member in a local nonprofit publisher, hosting prose workshops and mentoring writers. Jim's stories have appeared in Datura Literary Journal, The Wapshott Press, Remington Review, Rochak Publishing, and Adelaide Books.

Jim is a California resident with an interest of historical, literary and science fiction. He and his first wife's young poet wife enjoy a small town life in or at the San Francisco Bay area. Jim earned an MA in U.S. History. His professional career has included military service, bookkeeping, research, librarian and technical writing. Jim is an active participant in his community's literary organizations serving as a board member in a few of non-profit publishers, literary press ... and also with two or more. Jim's stories have appeared in Delta Literary Journal, The Wagsing, These Remington Review, Rocket Publishing, and Attitude Books.

Milton Keynes UK
Ingram Content Group UK Ltd.
UKHW040659040324
438882UK00001B/14